LOST

LOST

Scott Stein

LOST. Copyright © 2000 by Scott Stein.
All rights reserved. Printed in the United
States of America. No part of this book
may be used or reproduced in any manner
whatsoever without written permission
except in the case of brief quotations
embodied in critical articles and reviews.

This is a work of fiction. Names, characters,
places, and incidents either are the product
of the author's imagination or are used
fictitiously, and any resemblance to actual
persons, living or dead, events, or locales is
entirely coincidental.

Published by Free Reign Press, Inc.
Langhorne, Pennsylvania
First Edition: July 2000

Stein, Scott
      LOST / Scott Stein
Library of Congress Control Number 00-91516
ISBN 0-9701554-0-9

For Andee

Acknowledgements

For undying love and support, I am forever indebted to my parents, Cheryl and David Stein.

For work and words that continue to inspire and instruct, I would like to thank Lester Goran.

For numerous critical comments and extraordinary enthusiasm, I would like to thank my wife, Andee, as well as Jason Stein, Amy and Jared Boshnack, Valerie Block, and Todd Behrend.

For technical expertise and professional assistance, I would like to thank Jodi Vinaccia, Ron Schorr, Tal B. Marnin, Wayne Kellner, and Scott Brandt.

For making it through flight school, I would like to thank Michael Muglia.

Who will have pity on you,
        O Jerusalem?
Who will mourn for you?
Who will stop to ask how you are?

            Jeremiah 15:5

Chapter 1

It was the truth and there was no denying it. Jeremy Keller was being followed. At first he didn't quite believe it. Who gets followed in real life?

In the movies and on TV and even in books people are followed all the time—usually private detectives, who manage to spot the blue sedan in the rearview mirror the instant it begins to tail them and who always escape after the requisite high-speed car chase. But this was life. Jeremy wasn't a private detective and had, to the best of his knowledge, never been followed before. It isn't as easy as it seems on TV. He didn't know if he should look at the man, or talk to him, or ignore him. As with everything else, there is a real if undefined etiquette to being followed.

The man in the dark suit and red tie glanced at Jeremy from behind a magazine at the other end of the newsstand. It was a *Country House, Country Home*, the annual double issue devoted to shrubbery. The man was tall, with a bushy black mustache, and a rotund face and flat nose framed his sunken, narrow eyes. His pinstriped suit jacket was too small for his shoulders; he appeared to be forever shrugging in response to some unasked question. He wore black shoes with gold buckles and black tassels, and a silver ring with an orange stone on the pinkie finger of his left hand.

Jeremy was a bit shorter than the man and lean, with dark, almost black eyes, angular features, and high cheekbones. His faded jeans were ripped at one knee and frayed where they met his worn sneakers. He warmed his hands in the pockets of his blue hooded sweatshirt. It was cool for late September, and the pleasant afternoon breeze had taken on a more aggressive attitude. The sun was shining bright in the cloudless sky.

There were others at the newsstand and on this first Sunday of autumn the Manhattan sidewalk was dense with people rushing to catch the bus or strolling arm in arm, carrying shopping bags with exclusive logos or hot dogs from the corner vendor and talking about the football game or upcoming local elections. A dog barked. The man resumed his reading, and seemed to pay Jeremy no attention.

Jeremy couldn't think of a reason for anyone to follow him. He was involved in no clandestine romances, had no radical political affiliations, nor moderate ones for that matter, and his job hardly inspired the kind of effort following someone entails. He wanted to attribute the man behind the magazine to coincidence and his own overactive imagination, but could not; being followed had to Jeremy a feeling of inevitability.

In the context of a vision he had always had of his life and its meaning, being followed made an odd sort of sense. Watching interviews with celebrities and artists and political leaders on television, Jeremy often wondered what set them apart from himself and, try as he might, was unable to credit either chance or skill for their success and his own lack of real accomplishment. He knew that they were different from ordinary people, that there was something special about them, and sometimes as he lay in bed waiting for sleep to overtake him Jeremy experienced with cold certainty the depth of his own importance. He was convinced it was destiny that made people great, and if Jeremy's role in human affairs had not yet revealed itself to him, he would just have to have faith. He saw the man behind the magazine as a potential revelation; he had been waiting too long to believe that fate wasn't asserting itself here on his behalf.

Jeremy walked with self-conscious stiffness from the newsstand, pausing to look in shop windows and at advertisements on telephone kiosks. He fought the urge to check over his shoulder for the man with the bushy mustache, knowing that a mistake now could be costly. Jeremy walked around the block and returned to the same corner, catching along the way an occasional glimpse of the man trailing him. He crossed a street and then crossed right back, and the man followed him, the expression on his face indicating nothing aside from a mild boredom. Jeremy went into a bookstore, where he stayed long enough to read the back cover of the newest best-selling thriller: *The Bailiff's Wife.*

In Baron Simon's latest spine-tingling novel in the Bailiff series, Anson Borelli uncovers a plot to assassinate the President of the United States during crucial upcoming Middle East peace talks. His investigation reveals a web of deceit and unearths evidence that even those closest to the President are conspirators. No one can be trusted. Only Borelli can save the President. Millions of lives are at stake. It will take all of Bailiff Borelli's training and courage to stay alive and avert a war. The conspirators are ruthless and have thought of everything, but when they kidnap the Bailiff's wife they commit the greatest mistake of all—they make Bailiff Anson Borelli angry! Soon to be a major motion picture!

Jeremy wasn't much of a reader, and left the store, the man with the bushy mustache not far behind. Finally, and slowly, Jeremy headed back to his apartment. He was tired from the day's effort; although it takes no great skill to be followed, it does take patience. As Jeremy approached his four-story red brick building, the man climbed into a yellow cab and was gone. Working his way up the steep marble stairs to his one-room apartment, Jeremy at once both sighed in relief and shuddered at the confirmation of what he'd suspected since first seeing the man that afternoon. He was being followed. It was the truth and there was no denying it.

Chapter 2

Morning came with the thunder. A heavy, blowing rain battered the window above Jeremy's bed and the still dark sky crackled with electricity, but he didn't awake until the knocking on his front door turned to banging. He sat up in bed for a minute, rubbing his eyes and breathing deeply in an attempt to gather his wits; the vague, lingering impression of an interrupted dream muddled his thoughts. Jeremy tried hard to recall the dream, but could not, and its meaning was lost to him. He pulled on a T-shirt and a pair of jeans, tip-toed barefoot across the wood floor, and looked through the peephole.

The super, Mr. Valkof, squat and in his early fifties, whose peculiarly arched eyebrows made it seem as if he were perpetually looking down on the rest of the world, even though he was a head shorter than Jeremy and probably never really looked down on anyone aside from the even squattier Mrs. Valkof, again pounded the door with the palm of his hand. "Mr. Keller, are you awake?" He spoke in earnest with an accent that Jeremy could identify only as European, with pronunciations hard and guttural. Jeremy undid the chain and the bolt and opened the door, his eyes blinking rapidly as they adjusted to the fluorescence of the hallway.

"This came for you," Mr. Valkof said, extending a thick manila envelope. He wore black slacks supported by black suspenders, construction work shoes, and a flannel sweatshirt. "Sorry to bother you this early, but we're going to be away all day—at my wife's brother's—and it looked important."

"No bother," Jeremy said, without conviction. "I didn't hear my bell."

"We were going to have a picnic, but this rain doesn't look like it's ever going to stop," Mr. Valkof said.

"Who delivers packages this early?" Jeremy asked, rubbing his eye.

"Oh," Mr. Valkof said, "no company I know of. I found it on the stoop." Then with a glance at his watch and a sigh, "I hate driving in the rain. I guess we'll just sit around and look at pictures again. My brother-in-law snaps with his camera at everything. He has a whole book of squirrels. He even labels them: 'Squirrel in tree' or 'Squirrel with nut.' My wife says he's an artist, but I think maybe he's a little crazy. But he's her brother, and you know how it is with family."

Jeremy nodded that he knew and thanked Mr. Valkof before retreating into his apartment. He bolted the door immediately, then examined the package. On its face in blue ink was Jeremy's name and address, but there was no postmark or anything else to indicate its origin. The mysterious handwriting and the prior day's events made him reluctant to open it, and Jeremy showered and dressed for work, fully aware as he buttoned his white shirt and knotted his navy blue tie that an explanation might be waiting for him inside the solitary envelope sitting atop his imitation mahogany dresser. That was precisely what he feared.

During Sunday's long night, as he had searched his memory for clues and hoped perhaps for a moment of divine inspiration to uncover the purpose of his existence, Jeremy had avoided considering the possibility that the man had some reason for following him unrelated to destiny. But confronting Monday's reality of the envelope in his possession unleashed familiar doubts—he had displayed in his thirty years no inclination toward the extraordinary— and an anger at his own powers of perception; he believed a degree of innocence was required in order to achieve greatness. Devotion not to posterity but to painting made the painter great, to writing made the writer, Jeremy thought, and he longed to lose himself in something other than a preoccupation with his own importance. But Jeremy didn't have a medium through which to reach out to eternity, had none of the artist in him, and could claim only the acute ability to see every occurrence as being somehow significant. This forced self-awareness wasn't what Jeremy would call a prescription for immortality. If anything, it was holding him back; a watched pot never boils, or so his father had told him.

How long he sat on the black cushion of his futon, staring from across the room at the package, he didn't know, but by the time the rattling at his door broke the spell of the manila envelope's strange writing and clear tape, the remaining darkness outside his window was the result only of clouds and the continuing rain. Jeremy walked softly to the door and checked through the peephole—someone was hunched over, playing with the lock. Even from this angle Jeremy recognized the man with the bushy mustache.

A fleeting panic turned to anger, then to caution. Whatever Jeremy's destiny might be, he still had rights, and he considered calling the police. They could never get there in time. He thought next of hiding behind the door, maybe with his heavy flashlight or a knife from his silverware drawer, poised to strike. But he remembered that he was not dealing with a small man, and it occurred to him that anyone who specialized in following people and picking locks would likely be capable of defending himself. Maybe he should just sit on his futon and wait for the man to open the door, then calmly ask him what he wanted. That the man had some sinister intention remained a possibility, and the notion that it might be Jeremy's destiny to be murdered in his own apartment crossed his mind. He decided that it would be best to avoid a confrontation.

It was not a simple matter to locate the key to the padlock securing the window guard leading to his fire escape, and as Jeremy fumbled through the top drawer of the old, beat-up desk adjacent to his kitchenette, he managed to be thankful that his search did not have to take place amid a blazing fire and blinding smoke. He flipped quietly through nearly two dozen keys on semi-rusted rings, some belonging to one of his three previous apartments, others to his mother's place upstate, still more which seemed to fit nothing and brought to his mind no recollections of days gone by, existing solely, he thought, to illustrate the sudden confusion of all things pertaining to his life. The fluttering in his stomach increased in intensity along with the rattling from just outside his front door, but then Jeremy found the key that he knew matched the window guard's padlock.

He closed the desk drawer and slid the manila envelope into the left front pocket of his long, beige raincoat. Although the key turned easily, it was with a measure of surprise that Jeremy unlocked the guard and swung it open—he was becoming accustomed to the unexpected. He stepped out onto the fire escape and into the rain, closed his window and the guard behind him, then made his way down the slick stairs. The gusting wind mocked his small black umbrella, turning it inside out and finally twisting its frail metallic frame until it looked a little like a bird with a broken wing. Jeremy deposited it in a nearby trashcan, pulled his coat tight, and resigned himself to his soaked head as he hurried up the block to the bus stop. There were no available seats on the bus, but Jeremy smiled with discreet satisfaction as he held on to the overhead rail and looked out the window; the bus was on its way, and there was no sign of the man with the bushy mustache.

Chapter 3

The mailroom was shrinking on an almost monthly basis. At one time referred to with a certain respect, even by those who had never actually been to the fifth floor, as the Message Center, because the nearly five hundred employees of Dubasky and Cohen, Inc. were then completely dependent on it for interoffice communication, the mailroom had not too recently become just that—a room for mail. E-mail had finally all but ended the endless trail of paper memos and notices that once covered every desk, and computer efficiency and downsizing had a year earlier eliminated a hundred and fifty jobs, twelve from the mailroom alone. As desks were cleaned out, the rows of cardboard boxes containing thirty years of design and account history extended progressively further from the wall opposite the long windows in the mailroom, the last evidence of a vanishing era, awaiting conversion into codes and bits of data.

Jeremy was one of six people still working in a remaining

corner of the large, dusty mailroom, a feat he attributed to having made himself indispensable to his supervisor. Each morning consisted of cutting and fitting Styrofoam, packing and taping boxes, collecting and stamping envelopes, and calling bicycle messengers; the afternoons of more of the same, as well as sorting through incoming mail and delivering it to the three hundred employees occupying eight of the building's thirty-three floors. His mother, when asked, would only say, "Jeremy is with Dubasky and Cohen. They make toys." But Jeremy didn't feel the shame her reluctant answer implied, and took to his more routine duties with the same enthusiasm he displayed when wrapping Christmas gifts of expensive port or Tiffany crystal paperweights in bright red and green with bows on top for executives of the various retail toy chains. He watered the plants, paying extra attention to the drooping philodendron in its burnt sienna pot, separated the white and colored paper into their respective recycle bins, was always first to answer the phone, and went to the store whenever supplies of cardboard or tape ran low.

This morning Jeremy was twenty minutes late and dripping water when he threw his coat over the back of a folding metal chair. Running the three blocks from the bus stop to his office had not succeeded in keeping him dry and had left his shirt and khaki slacks wrinkled. No one else wore a tie in the mailroom, but Jeremy knew that first impressions didn't allow for second chances, and did everything he could to stand out from the crowd. He hadn't joined Dubasky and Cohen with the intention of working in the mailroom for long. Jeremy had studied marketing at Queens College, and though he'd quit twelve credits shy of his bachelor's degree, he was sure he could work for the Promotions Department. Writing slogans for pump-action water guns and thinking up jingles for the newest remote-control car couldn't be too difficult, and throughout his seven years in the mailroom Jeremy worked on various publicity and advertising campaigns, on his own time of course, periodically slipping his ideas in with the rest of the Vice President of Promotions' mail. That Jeremy had never received a response from the Vice President didn't discourage him. Destiny's bigger plans for him made his job and lack of recognition more than bearable. Even if Jeremy worked another seven years in the mailroom, he could console himself with the knowledge that something greater lay ahead.

After the morning rush of packing and calling and sending, Jeremy remembered his envelope, but was unable to find it in his coat pocket. He looked on the chair and beneath it, searched his coat again, thought for a moment that he had absentmindedly put it in his desk, and checked each drawer twice. No envelope. "Claude," Jeremy asked, "did you see the envelope that was on my chair?"

Claude was slow, and usually silent. Though his was a mild retardation, stuffing and sealing envelopes were the extent of his professional skills, and Jeremy had it from a reliable source that Claude had been hired more for public relations and political reasons than anything else. Company picnic speeches never lacked an inspirational anecdote about Claude, but more importantly, Claude's father was not only a shareholder of Dubasky and Cohen, but sat on the board. Claude's desk—a narrow table, really—was against the left wall, just a few feet from a window. He wore an open collar beneath his knitted vest and was slight and pale, with the blackest hair Jeremy had ever seen. The Empire State Building was usually visible from where Claude sat, and whenever he thought no one was around he stared at it, sometimes for twenty minutes or more without looking away. Admiring the tower and its cloud-piercing needle always made him smile, a queer smile, as if the immensity of historic steel and glass spoke to him some private words of comfort and granted him over his impotence of thought and action a serenity that nothing else could provide. But today's storm denied him this view and its accompanying smile. A distinct scowl was Claude's only answer to Jeremy's question.

Jeremy asked again, with strained pleasantry, "Claude, did you see my envelope? I left it right here, in my coat pocket."

Claude didn't look up from his stack of letters.

"Claude, where is it?" Jeremy asked.

Claude said nothing.

"Claude, that envelope is very important."

Silence.

Now Jeremy was yelling, "What the hell did you do with my envelope? Where the hell is it?"

Claude swiveled to face Jeremy, his pursed lips articulating only an airy whistle, his dammed answer verging on the futility of release. Claude's pale face reddened, and then he ran from the room and his silence, faster than Jeremy would have guessed he could move. Jeremy was still for a moment, an appropriate response at first eluding him—then he heard the door to the staircase slam shut. Claude was familiar with the railroad and subway, coming to and going from work without assistance, but he never left in the middle of the day, and Jeremy had never seen him this agitated. When Jeremy reached the stairwell Claude was not to be found.

It is true, given the size of the city and the variety of

possibility open even to the most rational, that Claude could have gone almost anywhere. But in the story Jeremy was endlessly writing in his mind, nothing happened without some purpose, even if that purpose were hidden, for a time. Moreover, events when filtered through Jeremy's microscope of me never remained disconnected from his own destiny, even if they bore no immediately discernible relation to his life. If it all seemed random, that was due to a failure of imagination and interpretation. Jeremy had no lack in these areas, and even if he didn't know yet what everything meant it was encouraging to him that at least he knew they meant something. In his vision of the significance of events Jeremy was unable to see Claude's quiet outburst as anything but a piece of his own puzzle. This incident with Claude was only the latest in an existence fraught with opaque messages. Now, seeing the strings of Claude's fate wrapped intimately with his own, Jeremy felt the hold of chaos loosening. It made sense, to him. The man following him, the envelope, Claude. Events were happening too fast to not be coming to a head. As the meaningful and symbolic ascended in Jeremy's world past the aimless and uncertain, he knew that Claude could only have gone to one place—the Empire State Building. That's where Claude had to be. And that's where Jeremy went.

It continued to rain during Jeremy's five-minute cab ride to what had once been the world's tallest building. Twins dedicated to trade and a tower in Chicago named for a department store chain had long ago robbed Claude's obsession of some of its status, but Jeremy thought that the Empire State Building maintained its majesty despite, or even because of, its fall from the ranks of the loftiest. It was old, the first tallest building, the first at least worth recognizing, and he told the cab driver as much.

"No one will forget it," Jeremy said.

"What's that?" the cab driver asked, his English words fighting for clarity with his native accent.

Jeremy, guessing he was Dominican, not long in New York, spoke slowly to be understood, "The Empire State Building. I think it has more claim to fame than the Twin Towers or the Sears Tower. It was first."

"The Twin Towers are bigger," the cabbie informed him.

Jeremy couldn't disagree, and resorted to the movies to make his point. "But, when King Kong came to New York, what building did he climb?"

"The Twin Towers," the cab driver said, not aware of the original film but only the remake, in his misunderstanding happy that his passenger agreed with his taste in skyscrapers. It was impossible to predict what might result in a larger tip, but the talkative ones, not the ones who yelled, but the ones who spoke to him like they knew him, tended to give a little more. As if their talk and their money effectively bridged the Plexiglas chasm that separated them, eliminated the distinction between riding in the back seat and giving orders, and sitting up front and taking them. Jeremy had no such ulterior motives. He experienced none of the prevalent awkwardness between the servant and the served, and talked sincerely to the cab driver simply because he thought that the Empire State Building deserved respect, that its greatness shouldn't be forgotten just because something bigger had come along.

In a way Jeremy respected Claude's insanity, for its taste, for its acknowledgement of the importance of the past. It didn't occur to him that maybe Claude had never even been to the Empire State Building, that at his parents' home on

Long Island his insanity was just as happy staring at the spruce in the backyard, that had he worked in Chicago in a building facing the right direction, he would have spent most of his time paying silent homage to a tower inspired by a department store best known for its home appliances and discount tools.

There wasn't time to continue the debate with the cab driver, and Jeremy gave him a dollar tip and headed straight to the elevators inside the Empire State Building lobby. Though the rain had let up slightly, the outdoor observatory remained closed. No one was in the enclosed viewing room just below the building's giant spike either; visibility was still poor. In the dark viewing room Jeremy pressed up against the glass and strained to look out over the city, but could hardly make out even neighboring buildings, and was disappointed to have gained no startling insights from the top of the world. Jeremy felt for a second that he was being watched, but knew that there was nowhere for anyone to hide. He returned to the lobby.

Claude should have been at the top of the Empire State Building, but wasn't, and Jeremy was angry with himself for misreading the meaning of things. The properly dramatic scene he had anticipated, in which Claude had to be restrained from leaping from the observatory to his death, with Jeremy as the hero—of course—was not to be. Fate seemed to be teasing him with missed opportunities. Jeremy sensed the ever-lurking threat of doubt, but reminded himself that understanding destiny was not an exact science. Claude was, after all, retarded, and couldn't be relied upon to grasp the importance of symbolism. That had been Jeremy's error—thinking others had the same abilities of perception that he possessed. He resolved not to make the same mistake in the future, and his faith in his impending epiphany was restored.

Jeremy recalled an early morning in this same lobby, how long ago he wasn't certain, but he guessed close to twenty years, since his father had been alive then. Jeremy, his older brother Marc, and their father had visited the Guinness Book of World Records Museum, tucked away in a corner of the Empire State Building's lobby. The warmth and wonder of an idealized childhood washed over Jeremy as he remembered his first encounter with the wax likeness of the world's fattest man. Next to the representation had been a giant red hoop, suspended from the wall at hip's height for all to compare the fattest man's waist against their own. It had easily encircled the three of them at once, and their father's deep laugh echoing throughout the dimly lit museum had caused both sons to hide their faces and quietly, then more forcefully, shush him. Near the museum's entrance had been the wax statue of the world's tallest man, with his dignified brown suit and thick glasses and strained posture, seeming almost vulnerable in proportion to his eight foot eight inch height.

Jeremy felt an uncomfortable, sad nostalgia in contemplation of his father's awe of the place, and his own. They had both been struck by the notion that each person honored in the museum had managed a singular achievement, however odd. Perhaps Jeremy had really been impressed only afterwards, a result of his father's daily references to the lessons offered by the accomplishments listed in the Record Book, a copy of which he had bought at the museum. His father was attracted particularly to the man who held the record for lying longest on a bed of nails. That man, whose sole legacy was a mounted black and white photograph of him prone on a porcupine mattress, next to a note indicating an absurd number of consecutive days and nights, which Jeremy could not now recall, was emblematic to Jeremy's father of a determination that he himself aspired to possess. More even than determination it indicated an enthusiastic stamina, an ability to cheerfully withstand all things, to not so much suffer the slings and arrows of outrageous fortune as to embrace them.

But Jeremy's father had specialized in suffering, with a lifelong asthma problem, less treatable then, and his aspirations to a superhuman endurance were in vain. He was at the time of their visit to the museum a self-employed electrician, but soon after sought a more lucrative vocation when credit card collection agencies began calling more than once a day. He worked on commission for a year selling gold-plated bathroom fixtures door-to-door to wealthy residents in nearby Long Island, but wasn't much of a salesman, and gave it up for the steady income and job security of a toll booth clerk on the Throgs Neck Bridge.

His wife, a third grade teacher, concluded at about this time that she wanted more out of life. She refused to lead the kind of stagnant existence her parents had led, and urged him to find a higher-paying career. She thought he was lazy and a failure, and told him so. But he believed that if something were meant to be, if he were supposed to make more money, it would happen, and nothing he or anyone else did could bring it on or ward it off. "All we have is each other" was his way of apologizing to his family for their regular dinner diet of macaroni and cheese. Mounting debts and inevitable bankruptcy didn't matter to him as long as they were together. It mattered to her, and she divorced him a month after he began collecting tolls. He found a small apartment, and worked as much overtime as they would let him, because he worried about what his ex-wife might be telling his children about him, and wanted above all for his sons to look up to him. He died a week before Jeremy's thirteenth birthday, an asthma attack induced by rush-hour exhaust fumes on the Throgs Neck Bridge.

Jeremy hadn't been to the cemetery where his father was buried in more than five years, and felt the sudden need to see the Guinness Book of World Records Museum. He asked the woman in the neat blue uniform behind the information desk where he could find it.

"I'm sorry, sir," she said. "That museum is no longer in the Empire State Building."

"Really? When did it move?"

"Just a year or two ago," she said.

"No big deal," Jeremy said. "Where can I find it? Downtown?"

"No. It's moved back to London."

"London?" Jeremy asked.

She nodded. "Sorry. But we do have a new flight simulator on the third floor, with the latest interactive technology, if you're interested."

He wasn't. Jeremy thanked her and wandered outside. It was just as well, he thought. The past had its limitations, and he needed to concentrate on the present, and his future. Jeremy, for one, wasn't going to lie on a bed of nails waiting for something to happen in his life.

Chapter 4

Jeremy walked in the light rain. The weather improved with each intersection he traversed—surely an omen of his good fortune. A feeling of freedom grew in him with his increasing distance from the Empire State Building, and an unexpected joy, all the more joyful for its unexpectedness. He couldn't explain its cause, but then he never could. He'd had so many moments of doubt that taken together they comprised an entire lifetime. But the joy of certainty, which it was his gift to feel in the unguarded moments in-between life, visiting him in gaps and starts when it willed, as it did now, was compelling enough to bolster his peculiar idea of himself. In his disquieting euphoria Jeremy thought he understood how a man might take himself for a prophet. Indeed, the world made a sense to him in this state—to his eye objects moved more slowly, sounds that normally drifted past without making themselves understood now waited to be heard before becoming one with the atmosphere.

He walked a steady stride, seeing emptiness on faces he

passed on the crowded street. It wasn't emptiness in the sense of blankness. It was an emptiness that came from being too full, too occupied: the man in the Italian suit, intent on getting the gum off the bottom of his shoe, leaning against a lamppost and clutching the stringy, black-red end of it with his fingers; the woman late for her interview, running as fast as her too-high heels would let her but stumbling every few steps, never noticing the rip in her stocking; the dozens of people on this block alone plunging headlong into the next minute without thought for the minute they were in, or the one just past. They were so busy living they seemed to Jeremy to not be alive at all. Sometimes he thought that he was the only one who knew that there existed something more important than their daily lives, even if to date he hadn't discovered what it was.

Jeremy stopped at the display window for Strawberry Dreams, a specialty shop featuring exotic varieties of strawberry from around the world. They sold yogurt, milkshakes, ice cream, shortcake, jam, anything really that included strawberries in its composition. Strawberry pancakes were available, and waffles with fresh strawberries on top, and strawberry syrup—never, heaven forbid, plain maple. The shop was new, or at least Jeremy had never heard of it. Shops—they preferred to be called boutiques—like these were popping up all over the place. Coffee bars dominated the Manhattan landscape, and it seemed that everyone with a little cash to spare was gambling it on finding the next big trend. There were boutiques devoted entirely to organic food, pasta, nuts, wine—the narrower the focus the better. Give people the badge of exclusivity, like the coffee bars had, make sure they knew how cutting edge their tastes were, how avant-garde their sensibilities, and money, lots of it, would follow.

Strawberry Dreams held an instant and particular fascination for Jeremy. He was terribly allergic to strawberries, and hadn't tasted one since the cake on his fifth birthday, an indiscretion on his parents' part that had resulted in a trip to the emergency room. Strawberries were the forbidden fruit, and as such commanded attention. But Jeremy wouldn't eat one. The consequences, his mother had told him (he had no recollection of his fifth birthday, nor any before the age of ten), included a numbing of the jaw and difficulty breathing. Fortunately, food wasn't especially important to him. He wasn't one of those people who began thinking of dinner while taking the last bites of lunch.

There were eight elevated pink tables each with four red chairs in Strawberry Dreams. The main decor consisted of personified cartoon strawberries painted on the walls—five with exaggerated dimples were picking strawberries from a tree with their stubby arms. One, with a crown on his head, lay on a golden couch, looking very much like a king from an old low-budget comedy sketch, the kind Johnny Carson used to do on *The Tonight Show*. This sense was reinforced by one-dimensional pillars and the stone ruins of a coliseum painted in the background. The strawberry king's impudent, puckish expression reminded Jeremy of Dom Deluise. King Strawberry was being hand-fed a bunch of strawberries, as if they were grapes, by another cartoon strawberry, an overdrawn flirty woman with long eyelashes, longer legs, and bright lipstick.

Inside Strawberry Dreams Jeremy's inexplicable joy met its cause. Behind the pink counter, which projected into the room in the outline of a strawberry, and wearing a floppy chef's hat with a repeating red strawberry pattern, was Brooke. Jeremy had guessed she was a Brooke before he saw the strawberry nametag pinned on her apron, or at least later believed he had. He was grateful to whatever force in himself had made him walk these streets and enter this boutique. He knew that it had directed him here, to this place, to meet her.

Brooke was wiping the counter down with a rag. She was short, just over five feet, with waves of brown hair and wide, browner eyes. Brooke had perfect teeth, a pretty, full-cheeked face, and a permanent, startled look, like a deer caught eternally in the headlights of an oncoming car. When she smiled, which Jeremy immediately knew she did at all times, she was beautiful. She threw the rag into the sink and began slicing strawberries with a wood-handled serrated knife. Jeremy was standing at the counter now, and Brooke looked up.

"What's your strawberry dream?" she asked, not embarrassed at the words as they passed her perfect teeth, the phrase uttered so often by her that it seemed natural.

Jeremy was silent.

"Can I get you something?"

Jeremy wasn't prepared to talk to her, didn't know what he could possibly say, and pretended to look over the menu hanging on the wall behind the counter. He faked indecision, stroking his chin and squinting his eyes as if deep in thought.

"How 'bout these?" she suggested, placing a plastic basket of strawberries on the counter. The strawberries were grotesque and plump, each the size of a small apple. Only three of them fit in the basket.

Jeremy was still incapable of speech, so he bought the basket with a nod of his head. Brooke took his money, gave him change, and handed him a sturdy white paper bag with

King Strawberry on its side. She smiled the whole time, even as she spoke.

"Keep dreaming," she said, as if she had said it a thousand times before but meant it anyway.

Jeremy left Strawberry Dreams and took a deep breath. He wanted to stay all day, to hide behind a newspaper and catch glimpses of her as she cleaned tables and smiled and scooped ice cream and smiled and wished people strawberry dreams and smiled. But he had been gone from work for almost an hour, though it felt longer to him, and had to get back before he was missed.

On the street corner was a thin white man with a filthy flaxen beard, no more than thirty years of age. Hanging around his neck from old, knotted shoelaces was a cardboard sign. *WILL WORK FOR FOOD* was written on it in meticulous black print. The man shook a paper Starbucks coffee cup, jingling the coins he had collected and making sure to look all passersby directly in the eyes. Jeremy handed him the bag with the three five-ounce strawberries and wished him luck, then got into a taxi. The man reached into the bag, digging around the basket as if in search of buried treasure, but found nothing aside from the kind of strawberries that in a certain mind might inspire a B-horror movie. As Jeremy's cab pulled away from the curb the man hurled the basket of strawberries at it, then cursed. It was unclear to those around the man if he was cursing at the cab's passenger or at the inaccuracy of his own pitching arm.

Jeremy usually went weeks without taking a taxi—the bus and subway met his daily needs, and the mailroom, despite his years of service and indispensability, didn't pay enough for him to throw money around. Today was no ordinary day, though, not with Jeremy's envelope and Claude's escape and Brooke, and he had hailed the cab without financial compunction. He knew that the proximity of his date with destiny would lay waste to his monetary concerns.

By the time the cab made the left to go downtown back to his office, Jeremy knew that he loved her. Brooke. The name was perfect, too. He could see her smile when he closed his eyes, but struggled to see the rest of her. Their encounter had lasted only a minute or two, and now was a blur to him. He remembered that she had black hair, so dark that her smile in his mind was even brighter. And her eyes, now that he thought about it, couldn't be brown. His own eyes were brown, and that wouldn't do for Brooke. Were they green? Reflected in the mirror of memory he knew they must be, and her green eyes became a fact to him as incontrovertible as the azure sky, as certain as his love for her and the inevitability of her love for him.

The cab was stuck in traffic at the beginning of the block, and since Jeremy could see his office building and the rain had all but stopped, he paid the fare and walked up the street. His fear that something horrible had happened to Claude, suppressed until now by his concern for his own destiny and the remembrance of his youth and his father, then by Brooke, found justification in the cause for all the traffic on the block—a fire rescue truck, parked in front of his building. There was no smoke to be seen billowing from an office window, no flashing lights or piercing siren from the truck, and, aside from pleading horns from backed up cars, no indication that anything out of the ordinary was happening. Jeremy didn't want to look to the roof—he felt guilty for the selfishness of his earlier desire to save Claude from a plummet from the Empire State Building observatory, mixed with a fresh, guiltier desire, that he tried without success to wish away, to see the heroism of his dramatic premonition come true here on this smaller stage. It didn't—no one was on the roof.

The building was designed in the most modern style. Its twin automatic revolving doors turned continually, but silently, and the narrow lobby, with its slanting blue glass to the wider second floor, seemed to challenge the laws of physics by the inverse logic of its proportion. The exterior lobby glass reflected too much sunlight for the tree inside the lobby to be a real one, but it was a remarkable facsimile. Helping the illusion was the subtle, barely perceptible whistling of two birds, maybe three, produced by speakers hidden in the branches of the tree. Jeremy entered the building. The hall on his right contained the three passenger elevators. Building administration had an office in the hallway on his left, and by the entrance to this hallway, just outside the door to the women's restroom, were six firefighters and Frank, Jeremy's supervisor from the mailroom.

Jeremy thought of Frank more as a brother than a supervisor. They had in common a loyalty to the company and each other, and a seriousness about their work. It was Frank who had made sure Jeremy kept his job when the company restructured, even though there were others with seniority that had to be let go. The first Friday of every month, and sometimes the third as well, Jeremy and Frank went to the pub around the corner from the office after work. They'd always share a pitcher of beer and play a few games of Foosball. Jeremy admired Frank because Frank had found his destiny—running a mailroom—and embraced it. Not everyone was meant for great things.

Frank wore black sneakers, navy blue cotton pants, and a tan dress shirt buttoned to the top. With his ever-present utility belt and green multi-pocketed vest he resembled a soldier off to war—ready for any contingency. He was armed well for the daily fight against deadlines and last minute decisions—razor and tape measure at his side, stapler and packing tape each in its own holster, plus his beeper and other essentials hidden in pouches and pockets and leather compartments: scissors, paper clips, rubber bands, staple remover, indelible black marker, yellow highlighter. Jeremy couldn't remember ever having seen Frank at work without his clipboard, with the master list of each day's assignments, which he wielded when he spoke like an exclamation point; to Frank every statement required a physical punctuation. Had he shouldered a rifle and a backpack containing dried food and camping gear he couldn't have looked more prepared or alert. Frank's eyes roved as if winning the battle depended on his ability to see everything at once. To him work was a war, even if he was granted command only over five grunts, even if the mission—running a mailroom—seemed to others to lack the potential for glory.

Jeremy approached them.

"Where the hell you been?" Frank asked Jeremy.

"Lunch. What's going on?"

Frank waved his hands and rapped his clipboard with his knuckles as he said, "What's going on? What's going on? I'll tell you what's going on. Claude disappeared. That's right. I went up and down this building, looked on every floor. I tell you, I could've used your help. But we finally found him."

"He's in the women's bathroom?" Jeremy asked, incredulous.

"I've looked everywhere else," Frank said, "and it's

jammed shut. Where else could he be?"

"The women's bathroom?" Jeremy asked again.

"Yes, that's what I'm trying to tell you. We just found him." Frank smiled briefly at this triumph, his big front teeth crowded in his mouth, then wiped his brow on his shirt sleeve, his tired expression not unlike that of a man recently returned from combat and unable to find words to make others understand what he'd seen and felt.

The women's bathroom. Jeremy was disappointed no longer with himself but now only with Claude. Locking himself in the women's bathroom—it lacked not only imagination but also meaning. What point was there in hiding on a toilet?

"I tried to kick it in, but that door's steel, thick too," Frank said, taking a tender step to demonstrate his injured toe. "Not cheap either. I've been trying to get him to move the stuff blocking the door, but he won't answer me. We're gonna have to axe it."

"He hasn't spoken at all?" Jeremy asked.

"Not a peep."

"Maybe he isn't in there," Jeremy said, hopeful that there might yet be some meaning to Claude's disappearance.

Frank shook his head and laughed. "Oh, he's in there, Keller. He's in there. Alright boys, let her have it."

The firefighter with the axe, a broad-shouldered woman with long arms, took careful aim.

"Wait a second," Jeremy said. "Maybe he'll listen to me."

Frank was impatient. "Don't sweat it, Keller. I've got approval from the building and accounting. The door isn't *that* expensive."

But Jeremy knocked on the door anyway, and shouted, with as level a voice as he could, "Claude, are you in there?"

No answer.

"Claude, it's me, Jeremy. Can't we talk about this? Open the door."

Nothing.

"Look, Claude, I'm not angry about the envelope. I didn't mean to upset you."

"What envelope?" Frank asked.

"Oh," Jeremy said, "just an envelope that Claude took from my coat by mistake."

"Claude didn't take your envelope," Frank said.

"What?"

"I said Claude didn't touch any envelope. Some guy came, I think from International Sales, and took it while you were collecting outgoing. What did you say to Claude? You didn't yell at him, did you?"

"No, wait... Who took my envelope?"

"Forget your stupid envelope," Frank said. "What did you say to Claude?"

"Was he tall? Fat face, thick mustache?"

"Yeah. So?"

"Oh God," Jeremy said.

"He said it was his, that it wasn't ready to go out."

"Oh God."

"What did you say to Claude? Did you yell at him? What's going on, Jeremy?"

"Oh God."

"Open it up," Frank instructed the firefighter, pushing Jeremy out of the way.

The firefighter hacked with her axe at the doorknob. Steel screeched against steel, forcing the people in the lobby into silence and drowning out the chirping of the nonexistent birds in their fake tree. A crowd of twenty people in fine suits or the most fashionable skirts or white aprons with paper bags delivering lunch gathered around the firefighters, some concerned and others entertained, even reluctantly pleased, by this unexpected diversion in their day.

The firefighters fought their way into the room with a black battering ram. A small sofa was blocking the door, and a baby-changing table, but the firefighters smashed the door twice, and it swung open. Claude had piled all the paper towels and toilet paper he could find on the sofa, thinking that their added weight would make the door more secure. Rolls of paper and sofa cushions were scattered across the room as the door gave way.

Claude sat next to the sink on the tile floor with his legs extended, leaning against the powder blue wall—blood from his wrist thick like chocolate and running red into tile grooves, shards of broken mirror all around him. His breathing shallow, drool dripping from his chin, Claude stared blindly at the entrance to the bathroom, at the door hanging from its hinges, as if to look through it.

Chapter 5

Seven years of ignoring colds and flus and running errands in the snow, of paper cuts that were replaced by fresh ones before they'd had the chance to heal, of not looking co-workers in the eye on the elevator, of waiting to be acknowledged and hoping to be heard, of endless stifled ambitions, had been reduced to a cliché. "Clean out your desk" was all Frank said to Jeremy after Claude was rushed to the hospital.

Cleaning out his desk was a humbling and enlightening experience. It was amazing, the amount of crap Jeremy had accumulated in the course of seven years. He found a four-year-old invitation to the office Christmas party, two out-of-date calendars, wrappers for a brand of gum he didn't think was still available in the Western Hemisphere, and rubber bands. Whenever he had removed a rubber band from a delivery of incoming mail he stuck it in his bottom drawer. At first he had done this out of necessity, because he was never able to find one when he needed it. But it became a habit, and without thinking Jeremy had saved over the years 2,918 rubber bands. He counted them. With all the papers—he had kept periodic notes of his marketing ideas and rapid sketches of promotional in-store displays—and memos, among them birth announcements and deaths, promotions and raises, layoffs and restructurings, all Jeremy wanted to keep were the rubber bands. They were the only things he felt belonged to him. He had no use for 2,918 rubber bands, and many of them were streaked with black newsprint. Some had become intertwined with balls of dust and hair. But he took them home to his apartment and put them in the bottom drawer of the old, beat-up desk adjacent to his kitchenette.

All that was left from his seven years—for some species that was a lifetime—was a paper shopping bag full of rubber bands. Even dense and crammed into one bag their weight was inconsequential. Jeremy kept them precisely because of their pointlessness. All they did was take up space. That's all Jeremy had done for the last seven years, waiting for destiny to seek him out as if it had nothing better to do. The rubber bands were a reminder to him that nothing added to nothing amounted to nothing. He saw his sudden unemployment not as a setback but as an opportunity. The realization that he had spent forty-five hours of every week delivering other people's lives to them, that in all his time in the mailroom he had never received even a single letter, not even junk mail addressed to him, made him vow to pursue his destiny with renewed passion and vigor.

He returned home after being fired and emptying his desk to find everything as he had left it. If the man with the bushy mustache had succeeded that morning in picking his lock he had been equally successful in leaving no sign that anyone had been there. Jeremy decided not that the man and his envelope were unimportant, but that more immediate matters of karma took precedence.

   Claude's welfare was the most pressing. Besides the four years they had worked in the same room, and the genuine affection and concern he felt for Claude, Jeremy had no desire to be even partly responsible for the death of innocence. He called his office all late afternoon into early evening to find out if they had any news. They hadn't heard from the hospital, and after his tenth call in three hours, Frank got on the line and told him never to call them again. Jeremy phoned the hospital and got their voicemail system. The recorded voice of a woman, obviously reading from a script, with an accent he couldn't place, welcomed him and instructed him to press 1 if it were an emergency, then the # button. He pressed 1 and #. A man, a live, hoarse voice, sounding as if he had been born smoking a cigarette, picked up the line a few seconds later and asked Jeremy what the problem was, who had been hurt, where they should send the ambulance, and what insurance they had. Jeremy told him about Claude and asked to be connected to someone who could tell him what his condition was. The voice told him that this didn't qualify as an emergency, admonished him for putting lives in danger by pressing 1 for emergency when in fact no emergency existed, and reconnected him to the voicemail system.

   The recorded voice of a woman, obviously reading from a script, with an accent Jeremy still couldn't place, welcomed him and instructed him to press 1 if it were an emergency. He didn't press 1. He could press 2 if he wanted to speak to a representative from the gift shop, 3 to be connected to the hospital's official flower delivery service, 4 to hear from an insurance representative, 5 for paid experimental programs through the university, 6 for the hospital pharmacy, 7 for public and community relations, 8 to find out about donating blood, 9 to find out about donating organs, 10 for information about counseling groups for drug addicts, 11 for support groups for the children of drug addicts, 12 for information about counseling groups for alcoholics, 13 for support groups for the children of alcoholics, 14 for information about counseling groups for smokers, 15 for support groups for the children of smokers, and 16 to inquire about the condition of friends or family staying in the hospital.

Jeremy pushed 1 and 6 and #, but must have slipped, because the voice told him he had selected 9, and asked him to confirm his interest in learning how he could donate his organs by pressing 1, or to press 2 to return to the main menu. He pressed 2. The voice thanked him for his interest and then made a passionate, monotone plea for his organs. It informed him that he could save dozens of lives, that he didn't need the organs where he was going anyway, that it was ecologically sound to recycle, that donating while still alive was preferable since many organs were redundant—the human body could function quite well with a single kidney or lung. It described in detail the happiness of little Tina Jankowitz, who could see because the generous little Enrico Hernandez had died in a six-car pileup on the Long Island Expressway but his eyes had survived. She saw with the eyes of a saint, it said, and her parents and Enrico's parents were now best of friends. It asked Jeremy to reconsider his selection of number 2, to have a heart for the Tina Jankowitzes of the world, and if that weren't reason enough, to remember that not only did donating organs almost guarantee admittance into heaven on the first try, but could be lucrative if the parts were in good condition and working order.

Jeremy pressed every button on his phone but couldn't escape the sales pitch, so he hung up and called again. The same recorded voice of a woman, even more obviously reading from a script, with an accent Jeremy would have wagered was Jamaican, welcomed him and instructed him to press 1 if it were an emergency. He could press 2 to buy overpriced coffee mugs with cartoon depictions of cats with stethoscopes around their necks, 3 to send allergy-provoking weeds to patients living in oxygen tents, 4 to finance his insurance agent's vacation to the Bahamas, 5 to be poked and prodded by stoned graduate students for six dollars an hour, 6 for discount drugs that were better than whatever he was getting on the street, 7 for propaganda, 8 to sell his blood for beer money, 9 to be scavenged and auctioned off to the highest bidder, 10 for friends to do drugs with, 11 to meet other kids with access to their parents' stash, 12 for drinking buddies, 13 for other kids with keys to their parents' liquor cabinet, 14 to quit smoking, 15 to quit secondhand smoking, and 16 to inquire about the condition of mildly retarded and severely distraught coworkers who had slashed their wrists with the jagged edge of a broken mirror in the women's restroom.

He carefully entered 16 and #, and a live voice, a man who sounded as if he had been smoking since the day he was born, asked Jeremy how he could help him. Jeremy told him about Claude and asked what his condition was. The man with the hoarse voice informed Jeremy that no information on that patient was currently available and thanked him for his call.

"Hold on just one second," Jeremy said. "I've been waiting ten minutes listening to the same message over and over. I need to know what's happened to him."

"I don't have that information, sir."

"Can't you ask someone? Doesn't anyone know?" Jeremy asked.

"I'm sure someone knows," the hoarse voice said. "I would imagine his doctor, maybe his family, the nurses. I would think they have to know."

"Now we're getting somewhere," Jeremy said. "Ask one of them how he's doing. I'll hold."

"I can't do that."

"Why not?" Jeremy asked.

"I can't leave my post. Who would answer the phone?"

"There isn't someone to cover for you?" Jeremy asked.

"There used to be, but with budget cuts and everything..."

"Can't you call one of the doctors to find out, or beep them?"

"I don't think I should. They're very busy."

"This *is* the number for information about patients, isn't it?" Jeremy asked.

"Yes."

"Then shouldn't you have information about patients?"

"That would make sense."

"Why don't you?" Jeremy asked.

"I don't have an answer for you."

"This is ridiculous," Jeremy said, feeling faint from the conversation.

"There's no reason to get all worked up," the man with the hoarse voice said.

"Of course there is."

"Don't yell at me. I just work here."

"I'm not yelling. Look, is there someone I can talk to, a

supervisor or something?"

"Sure. Let me connect you to my boss, in public relations. Have a nice day."

The phone rang and was answered on the other end. The recorded voice of a woman, seeming now to flow as if she were inventing the very words as she spoke them, with an accent Jeremy was sure was most prevalent in the west end of Kingston, Jamaica's capital, welcomed him and instructed him to press 1 if it were an emergency.

Jeremy pulled his phone out of the wall.

He took the subway to the hospital. Now that he was jobless he was in no position to be traveling by taxi, not three times in the same day. It was a clear night. Jeremy imagined as he walked to the subway station that if he had been anywhere but New York there would be stars visible in the sky. He knew that the light from the buildings and street lamps was the reason the stars couldn't be seen from Manhattan. He understood it rationally, knew of course that the stars were there despite his inability to see them, but still it made him uneasy. He wasn't against progress, was glad to have air conditioning and use escalators and watch television and all the rest, but couldn't help thinking there was something not quite right about blocking the heavens with neon lights and billboards advertising soft drinks.

Jeremy didn't mind taking the subway, especially since most of the graffiti had been removed. It was nice too to not be bothered by panhandlers every day anymore. The ad campaign urging passengers not to give money to beggars—it had suggested that their money would be better spent by donating to organized charities—and an increased police presence had been effective. There used to be homeless—they were never homeless people, just homeless—in every station, and it had been a rare train ride that didn't include some form of solicitation. There had been those who simply carried empty cups or held signs or quietly or not-so-quietly asked for money. But competition was as fierce in seeking handouts as in any business, and the American capitalist's spirit of ingenuity had once been as alive and well beneath the city's surface as it was above ground. A Hispanic woman used to sell batteries, a Chinese man little plastic Knicks key chains, a white woman with straggly hair packs of spearmint gum for a dollar each. She always wore a sign around her neck informing passengers that she was HIV positive and pregnant. She continued to use the sign without apology despite her failure over the months to show any evidence of her impending motherhood.

Jeremy didn't buy their batteries or key chains or gum, tried to avoid doing so on principle; there were beggars everywhere, and it wasn't possible to save everyone. If he gave to everyone who inspired pity in him there would be no end to it. But there was a black man Jeremy used to see on the train almost every morning singing *Strangers in the Night* and walking through the car with his baseball cap out. Man, could he sing. His voice was deep and rich and resonated. Passengers often clapped as he passed and gave him coins, even small bills. There was something about this destitute man in dirt-coated sweatpants with toes showing through holes in the front of his shoes singing about love at first sight. Jeremy always gave him a quarter or two, but usually felt guilty afterwards. It didn't seem fair that because this man could sing he had more right to a meal than other people. But Jeremy always gave to him just the same. A heavy woman, also black, used to read aloud from her Bible, shouting really, that the meek would inherit the earth, that all sinners would burn in hell. No one ever gave her money.

Then the city cracked down on quality-of-life offenses, and Jeremy no longer saw the man who sang *Strangers in the Night*, couldn't remember the last time he'd seen him. Jeremy did feel safer, he had to admit, and not having the guilt of refusing to give money to people who had hunger in their eyes, if not in their stomachs, was a welcome change. But he wondered, now that these beggars weren't on the trains anymore, where exactly they had gone.

Before entering the hospital's emergency room one had to wait in the waiting room. The waiting room embodied in its name the rarest of qualities—honesty. There was no euphemism here. The waiting room was for waiting, and in the waiting room of the trauma center there was always someone, no matter what time of day or night, in snow or rain, Christmas Eve or Fourth of July, waiting. Heart attacks, gunshot wounds, car crashes, and broken ankles had no respect for religion or patriotism. Today was no exception. There were a dozen people, in varying degrees of pain, sitting in gray plastic chairs arranged in a horseshoe, anchored to the floor and all connected by a steel beam that ran beneath them and kept the chairs from being thrown or stolen.

A nurse told Jeremy that patients would be seen first-come first-serve, with priority going to the most serious cases. His need to know Claude's condition was deemed a low priority, and he took a number from a dispenser like the kind used in a bakery, sat, and waited to be called.

A man with his shirt unbuttoned, revealing gray, matted hair on his chest, was trying to take even, deep breaths, but couldn't. His wife filled out an admission form while he continued, in his weak voice, to tell her that it was something he ate, indigestion probably. If she would only listen to him and cook with less onion, maybe take it easy with the garlic, he would be fine. It was a monster case of heartburn, was all. Even his forearms were sweating. She nodded as he spoke, tears in her eyes, not wishing to upset him further. Their number was coming up, after the next one, and he didn't need to worry. What was there to worry about? Just a monster case of heartburn, was all.

A woman and her son, a pudgy, freckled boy, sat in a corner. Fresh green paint stained his Nike T-shirt and jeans. He had a bump on his head. His mother held a clear bag with melting ice against the reddening bruise. The city would pay for what they'd done to her baby, she told him. In the morning she would call a lawyer, two lawyers, the ones who advertised on television late at night. He didn't have to worry. They didn't charge anything unless they won. And they would win. The top of that fence was slippery, that's all there was to it. It was a wonder more innocent people hadn't been hurt, even killed. No, she wasn't angry with him for climbing it. That fence had no business being there. It was an invitation for trouble. How could he have known it had just been painted and was still wet? He couldn't have, and that's why the city would pay. They would buy him a new shirt and jeans, too. Damn straight they would. And the city would pay for making him wait in this emergency room—was there no compassion in this town? Her lawyer would take care of it, though. She'd seen the commercials on TV. Her boy would get those braces after all. She couldn't wait to see that smile of his, once it was straightened out.

The feeling of despair from the couple waiting to find out exactly what had happened to their daughter clashed almost physically with the sterile optimism of long fluorescent bulbs running in twos the length of the ceiling. Where was the doctor? He had said only that their daughter wasn't out of the woods yet, that she had been shot. The girl's father muffled his sobbing with his hand. He stared at the floor. His wife's hand was on his head, rubbing the patch of soft skin no longer protected by a thin layer of hair, her face betraying neither sadness nor anger, as if by her refusal to react to events she could negate their reality.

The waiting room's walls were bright white and there were no windows. A television mounted in the corner of the room near the ceiling, visible only to one end of the horseshoe of chairs, was tuned to a local news show. The news anchor on the television, a blond man with a strong jaw and sharp chin, smiled. He shuffled the papers on the anchor's desk as he read from the teleprompter:

In the latest exclusive Channel 12 poll, 512 Americans just like you were asked to vote for the decisions you would make if you ran the country. You agreed overwhelmingly on lower taxes, more police, more money for researching a cure for cancer, less crime, better education, a strong military, a stronger economy, and an end to the deficit. Now if only we could get our politicians to agree...

Also in the news, startling new research today is indicating that male pattern baldness may be a thing of the past. Tracy?

Tracy was blonde and pretty, on both accounts less so than her co-anchor. Her acting was better than his, though, and she worked hard to look as if she were reading from the papers on her desk, with some success:

Thank you, Chad. Hair today, gone tomorrow? Not anymore. It's true! Throw out those rugs, dump the spray paint, lose the hat—you're hair to stay! Channel 12 has learned that scientists have developed a new pill that may once and for all put an end to those embar-

rassing bald spots and receding hairlines. The pills have been tested on bald rats and have been successful in reproducing hair. What does this mean for you? That's up to the FDA. No word yet on when the pills might be available to the public. Chad?

Thank you, Tracy. Some sad news tonight. We have a breaking story for you now, and it's another tragic case of youth violence. A teenager was shot down in cold blood as she walked home from school, just a few hours ago. It's a bizarre case—apparently the suspect or suspects filmed the crime, then delivered the tape to us. You'll see the exclusive video only on Channel 12. A word of caution—the video is unedited and quite graphic.

At this the grieving couple turned its attention to the television. The man looked at it through defensive, half-closed eyes. His wife opened her mouth, but said nothing.

COLD BLOOD appeared on the screen in black, red dripping from the C and the B, with a bullet shooting through the words, splitting the letters in two. This graphic was accompanied by the sound effect of a machine gun firing. Then the video came on.

It was difficult to make out the person on the video, which was in color, though it was clearly a girl, by her gait and posture a teenager. The video was being shot from a moving car. The car was creeping along in the same direction as the girl was walking. It stopped. A hand holding a gun was then visible at the bottom of the screen, aiming at the girl from the car. It was difficult to tell if the camera and the gun were being handled by the same person, but it seemed that they were, because the camera began to shake when the gun appeared. A voice from just behind the camera yelled, "Hey," and the girl turned to face the car. For a second the girl's face was clear. She was wearing glasses and had short, black hair.

In the hospital waiting room the girl's mother was wailing, pleading, "No, no, no, no, no, no."

Jeremy rushed to turn off the television, but was too slow. There was no remote control. He needed to stand on something to reach the controls on the television, but the chairs were bolted in place.

On the video the girl's expression changed, from surprised curiosity at being called to from a strange car to a disbelieving fear. Her face was only visible for a second, but it was a long one, and her mother in the waiting room was able to scream no a thousand times in her heart before the sound of a gun being fired came from the television, and the girl's head flung back and she crumpled to the ground. There was cheering and hooting from inside the car, and someone said, "Bitch," with an air of justification. Then the video ended.

Chad looked serious. Tracy was moved, and she brushed the hair away from her face before she spoke:

Police are confident that this video will provide important clues, and are hoping to make arrests soon. Anyone with information about this crime should call 800 GET THEM. As always, information leading to an arrest will be rewarded with a thousand dollars and an official Channel 12 GOT 'EM tote bag. No word yet on the girl's condition. More on this story as it develops. Chad?

Thank you, Tracy. We urge our viewers to get involved. Only you can make this a better world by putting an end to crime. Please call with any information. Even if you think it isn't important, the police want to hear from you.

Jeremy by this time had found a mop, sitting in a gray bucket of water by the entrance to the waiting room.

We're going to show the video to you one more time, this time in slow motion. Please pay close attention.

Jeremy tried to push the television's power button with the wood end of the mop, but the button was too small and the end of the wood handle too round. On the television the girl was again walking down the street, her steps exaggerated by the slow-motion effect. The gun was raised. The girl's mother screamed and her father tried not to look, but the girl continued to walk. Jeremy checked the end table, thinking that the remote control for the television might be hidden beneath a magazine. It wasn't. On the screen the girl turned, ever so slowly, to face the camera.

"No, no, no, no, no, no," her mother said.

Jeremy ran at the TV with the mop raised like a javelin. There was a crack and a fizzle as the screen was smashed by frayed and soiled strips of cloth followed by a wood handle. The mother stopped saying no, the father looked up at Jeremy. Everyone in the waiting room was silent. What had been a television was now an empty shell, a dead plastic beast with a spear in its side. The room smelled of smoke.

Jeremy ran out of the trauma center, almost reaching the subway station before hospital security arrived in the waiting room to find the remains of the television set.

The girl died that night.

Chapter 6

Jeremy avoided watching the news during the days following his visit to the hospital, and looked in the paper mainly to see if he could find information about Claude. Someone had managed to keep events at Dubasky and Cohen out of the news. Even they wouldn't be able to influence the obituary page, though, and after three weeks of morning walks to the newsstand to read Long Island newspapers, with no mention of a certain successful suicide, Jeremy was finally able to convince himself that Claude was still alive.

The obituary page was the part of the paper Jeremy read most regularly and diligently. People were remembered and honored and defined in print for the most ordinary things—the man responsible for pressuring the city into posting more stop signs than any individual in New York's history died on a Tuesday. He was credited with saving hundreds of lives. He wasn't killed ironically by a speeding car but died alone and anticlimactically in his sleep of pancreatic cancer at the age of fifty-four. Most people died the way they lived: uneventfully, quietly. That same day a woman went at ninety-nine. She had been, three years earlier, the oldest active librarian in New York City. Her life had been spent stamping books and alphabetizing books and telling children to keep it down while they read books and reading books herself, and she had slipped away in silence. Their lives in the newspaper resembled the stat line that followed a baseball game. No sense of the texture of the thing, of the subtleties of the game, just hits and strikeouts and bases on balls. They were the lucky ones. At least they rated a headline. For every feature article there were a dozen or more smaller listings, people whose lives were reduced to born and died on dates and survived by fill-in-the-blank. Most people never did anything worth recording, leaving the world untouched by their existence.

Jeremy didn't spend all of his unemployed time reading about the deceased. He looked through the want ads too, but found nothing he was qualified for in the three weeks since he'd lost his job. Severance pay had run out after the first two weeks, but Jeremy was collecting unemployment. It wasn't enough to pay his rent, though, and the small amount he had saved over the years would only last him another few weeks.

Visiting Strawberry Dreams was his primary activity, the only thing besides reading the paper that he did every day. He never said much to Brooke, only hello and whatever was required to place an order. He couldn't sit in the boutique for hours and look at her, either, because there was nothing sold in the place that he could safely eat. It would be suspicious if he came each day, ordered a plate of food, and never touched a bite. His only option was to buy something inexpensive to go. Jeremy always ordered a basket of strawberries—he didn't want her to have to slice or mix or do any other work for him, especially since he would just give the food away as soon as he exited the shop. This limited the time he had with her. He prolonged his visits by never having exact change, by asking her to break large bills, by leaving the counter without his change or his bag of food. Brooke would have to call him back with a smile. The basket of strawberries he always bought ran him $4.50. He felt guilty paying her, that he was using her. It cheapened their relationship. His time with her was a kind of chaste prostitution—$4.50 daily for a smile to make up for the absence of anything real in his life.

Jeremy exited Strawberry Dreams, clutching his paper bag close to him as he walked up the block. It wasn't always easy to give away the basket of strawberries. Most people on New York streets didn't look Jeremy in the eye, didn't look anyone in the eye, and usually ignored him as he tried to get their attention and offer them free of charge the exotic variety of fruit. They never looked up as they moved past him, counting on their speed and inconspicuousness to keep them safe. Those who did look him in the eye generally did so in defiance, silently challenging him to violate their space. Some of them clenched their teeth or fists. Others flashed deliberately insane smiles or talked out loud to themselves as if trying to convince him that they were even crazier than he was.

Jeremy never wanted to throw perfectly good if somewhat intimidating strawberries in the trash just because giving them away required effort on his part. He once walked fifteen blocks before finding the plump, red-headed woman willing to accept the basket from him. She had at first resisted, but Jeremy argued with her for five minutes, assuring her that the strawberries were not only safe but delicious. She'd had her doubts, and demanded that he taste one before she would take them. How did she know he wasn't some psycho handing out poisoned strawberries for kicks? She wouldn't fall for his ploy, refused to be the headline of tomorrow's *New York Post*: STRAWBURIED! He was lucky she didn't call the police, and would be best off if he just left her alone.

But Jeremy had patiently explained that he was allergic to strawberries, and told the woman that he only bought them because he had a crush on the girl behind the counter. Why should they go to waste? There were children somewhere starving to death. She finally consented after he showed her his driver's license and signed a note. She copied his name and address and underneath wrote the following on a crinkled napkin she had pulled from her pocketbook: *I promise that the strawberries have not been tampered with and therefore are safe.* She wasn't a lawyer, but was sure the note would allow the police to arrest him if he had done anything to the strawberries. Then she took the biggest, juiciest strawberry she'd ever seen out of the basket, and ate it down to its stem in a single bite, chunks of it tumbling down her face and shooting through the air like bullets as she told Jeremy how glorious it was. He remembered thanking her for her trust.

There were rare days when the first person Jeremy approached eagerly accepted the strawberries, and he hoped today would be one of them. Mid-October could be surprisingly cold, and he was in no mood for persuasions and negotiations. The piping of a flute from the corner, across the street from a subway station entrance and two blocks uptown from Strawberry Dreams, soothed him. Jeremy crossed over with his basket of strawberries.

Five dark-skinned men with black hair, dressed in modern versions of traditional American-Indian attire, complete with moccasins and feathers hanging from earrings and suede ponchos with frills on the arms and blue jeans, sat on upturned plastic milk crates, making music so beautiful it had attracted a crowd of at least thirty people. In front of the band was an open guitar case, dollar bills and silver coins on its interior red felt lining, either recent donations from listeners or displayed as a prompt for those who had yet to show their generous appreciation.

Pictured on a sign next to the guitar case, in the most advanced computer graphics, was a cartoon buffalo sitting behind the wheel of a convertible Cadillac. The buffalo was winking. Painted on the door of the black car speeding through the desert highway was the planet earth in blue and green. In big black letters above the car was the band's name: *Native Sons*. Those who looked close enough to read the writing beneath the Cadillac were instructed to *Save the Planet*. A young boy dressed in the same fashion as the musicians, with the addition of a feathered headdress, moved among the people, selling from a full wicker basket CDs with the same buffalo art work on their covers. The basket was hanging low like a kangaroo's pouch, from straps around the boy's neck, leaving his hands free to play his flute, which he put aside only to make an occasional sale.

Jeremy couldn't name all of the instruments the musicians were playing, but despite its slowed pace knew the song immediately as *Satisfaction*. In their hands it was a more peaceful tune than he remembered. He was drawn to the crescent of humanity swaying in time to the optimistic, soulful sounds that rose above the angry noise of the city. There was a feeling of togetherness among these people who didn't know each other, and Jeremy experienced for the first time in weeks a kind of calm, a relaxed contentment with himself that made him sigh, and smile. The guitar player strummed, and stomped his foot. A tall, thin man, eyes closed in passionate concentration, alternated blowing into his eight bamboo pipes lashed together; it sounded like no pipe Jeremy had ever heard, and made the hair stand up straight on the back of his neck.

A percussionist thumped barehanded on a pair of congas. Hanging on strings from a horizontal bamboo pipe were several dozen car keys, which when he ran his hand through produced by their gentle collisions the most mystical sounds. Another man had before him assorted upturned metal kitchen pots, three of varying size with long handles built for cooking pasta or soup or sauce, and a fourth oblong pot—a hospital bedpan. He used as drum sticks two spoons, a standard shining teaspoon and a larger wood one, more like a ladle. The fifth man played backup on a standard flute, taking the lead when the boy had to pause to collect money in exchange for a CD.

The boy was definitely less than ten years old. He danced as if he were circling a fire and praying for rain—lifting each knee high in turn and spinning with a grace belonging only to the young and unburdened. His twisting and gliding brought him to Jeremy, and he stopped playing his flute just long enough to hand over a CD, hopes for a sale flowing from him like the music that continued to attract people from all directions. Jeremy liked the graphic of the sly buffalo and his sleek, speeding Caddie. Listed on the back of the plastic case were the songs, six traditional pieces with names Jeremy couldn't begin to pronounce, and in addition to the famous tune by the Rolling Stones three modern popular songs: *When The Levee Breaks*, *It's Hard To Be A Saint In The City*, and *Maxwell's Silver Hammer*. In print so small Jeremy had to strain to read it, well below the list of songs, was the following: *All traditional Peruvian songs recorded in Peru.*

The boy held his hand out. "Fifteen dollars," he said.

Jeremy handed back the CD. "No, thank you."

"Fifteen dollars," the boy said, offering the CD.

"I don't have a CD player," Jeremy said. "Do you have any cassettes?"

"Fifteen dollars," the American-Indian child from Peru said, sticking the CD right under Jeremy's nose. There were no cassettes in the basket.

"I'm sorry," Jeremy said, and began to walk away.

The boy followed him, playing his flute and dancing in wide arcs around Jeremy, slowing his progress up the street.

Jeremy stopped. "I don't have a CD player," he said again.

The boy took no notice and danced in front of Jeremy, light on his feet as he played the song's bridge. Jeremy tried to walk—with agility the boy skipped to block his way. He went left—the boy was there. Right—there was no getting around him. Jeremy faked left and tried to go right, but the boy had been playing the game longer, and did not fall for this deception. Jeremy surrendered after five attempts to get past, each time prevented by the reflexes of the young flutist, who sprang like a cat to occupy the space Jeremy was trying to reach.

Jeremy pulled out an old dollar from his pocket. He held the money high in the air as he walked back to the crowd, to be sure that the boy and other band members saw it. He leaned over and took care that the wind wouldn't catch his dollar. Jeremy refused to be fate's pawn in some cosmic joke, rejected visions of himself chasing the green paper across the city as others laughed and the heavens rained down on him. The dollar bill landed without a sound on the soft lining of the guitar case, a silent victory.

The people still swaying to the music had a collective expression that frightened Jeremy. Their faces mirrored the ethereal music. He had been, moments earlier, swaying along with them and the waves of audible peace, but now didn't feel that he belonged. Whatever impulse had made him join them was gone, and he was alone again. The compulsion to lock arms with other people was foreign to him.

The crowd was a compendium of all humanity: poor and rich, women and men and children, representatives from every established ethnic group and others still undefined. There were red power ties with leather briefcases, aprons, skirts long and short, bicycles interrupted on their way to somewhere, jackets with *The Giants* on the back, the man with the bushy black mustache, a pretzel cart—

The man with the bushy black mustache—the man who had been following Jeremy, who had stolen the envelope from his office—he was there, in the crowd.

His expression differed from the rest; he wasn't even listening to the music, and stared at Jeremy without blinking.

Chapter 7

Jeremy and the man with the bushy black mustache just stood there, separated by twenty feet and a wall of people becoming one with the drifting beat of spiritual piping and jingling keys. The man did not look away, did not smile or nod, but remained intense and serious. He didn't blink for an unnaturally long time, and Jeremy's own eyes watered in sympathy. If breathing or a beating heart were to interfere with keeping an eye on Jeremy the man would have found a way around them as well. His gaze was level; his eyes didn't move. It was as if he were peering directly into the deepest part of Jeremy's soul.

The man appeared as calm as Jeremy did not. Jeremy's hands were shaking, his knees weak, overpowered by the rushing adrenaline. Evolution made people capable of fight and flight, enhancing their ability to do both when urgency demanded. Instinct didn't leave Jeremy options—he was a flight man all the way. If he were an animal wild and free on the plains of some dried-out continent or in a misty jungle, he wouldn't be the mighty lion or the fearless crocodile. He wasn't the tenacious hyena or the wild boar, either—both were dangerous when cornered and would strike if given no escape route. Jeremy was a kind of graceless gazelle. All he knew to do was flee. Even as the crocodile tightened its death grip on the gazelle's long neck and was dragging it to its murky end the gazelle galloped for freedom, in a panic and struggling with its last reserves of strength, but despite hearing its own neck break incapable in its innocence of causing or even wishing the crocodile any harm.

But running from the man with the bushy mustache at full speed was out of the question. It lacked dignity. Jeremy was an ambassador of destiny, and had to have some self-respect. Besides, he didn't want to give the man cause to do anything rash—he had no way to know if the man were armed, and in these situations knew that people were rather like dogs. They were provoked by sudden movements and liked nothing better than a good chase, an opportunity to bite the legs of frightened prey. Jeremy did flee, but as casually as his ready nerves allowed, walking unhurried, if a bit quickly, up the block. The man with the bushy mustache followed, his measured strides narrowing the gap between them in seconds.

The man was now only ten feet away and gaining ground. Sensing the man getting close, almost near enough to reach out and grab him, Jeremy tried not to panic. He saw a small corner grocery up ahead, with apples and pears and browning bananas in rows out front, and ducked into the doorway. If the man intended Jeremy physical harm, he would have to perform his evil deed before witnesses. The man did not rush into the grocery behind Jeremy, but stood just outside, peeking at him through the cleanest window in the city, above the orange signs with black writing announcing discounted beer and wine coolers and eggs and shaving cream in honor of Halloween.

The grocery was large, with shelves of household products to the ceiling around the store's perimeter. There were no bargain family-size packages. Everything sold in the place was aimed at people living in the city: microwave dinners and single-serving cups of ice cream in the back freezer, milk available in no larger than quart containers with caps color-coded for skim or low-fat varieties, miniature plastic jars of mustard and ketchup and cold medicine—even diapers only came five to a box. The store didn't cater to those who thought ahead. There wasn't space enough to offer larger versions and, more importantly, the profit on the smaller portions was greater. In one of these Manhattan stores a bar of soap or box of detergent could be nearly twice the cost of the same product in a supermarket in the other boroughs or on Long Island. It was the price people paid for living in the city that never slept.

By the grocery's entrance was a short deli counter displaying beneath its spotless glass slabs of processed meats in plastic wraps, and there were two food bars in the rear of the store, one containing cold salad and the other hot entrees. Stacked high in three columns on a small table between the two food bars were clear, ridged containers. A sign above this small table announced that the rate for the salad bar was $3.59 per pound and $4.25 per pound for the hot-food bar. There were three people in the store. A black woman at the salad bar placed Brussels sprouts with tongs into her container. She took minuscule carrots and baby corn and some sliced cucumber and went to the register at the counter by the front of the grocery.

An older Korean man wearing a white apron was dusting off the midget boxes of frosted cereal, using a pale blue stepladder to reach the shelf. He had watched the black woman carefully as she built her salad, as if he were half expecting her to dump the bucket of sprouts into her pocketbook and make a run for it. A teenage Korean girl took the woman's salad, strapped it tight with a red rubber band, and placed it on a shining chrome scale next to the register. The scale's green digital readout informed all who cared to look that the woman had .43 of a pound of food. She paid and left the store. The girl behind the counter had a round face with deep dimples. She wiped the immaculate scale down with a rag. The white floor had recently been waxed. Jeremy was reminded of an old commercial—he could see his vague reflection in the sparkling tiles. It was without doubt the cleanest grocery in the entire city.

Plenty of these grocery stores were owned by non-Koreans. But the stereotype was in this case based on truth, and many of the stores were indeed Korean-owned. Jeremy saw nothing wrong with this. Someone had to own them. Why not the Koreans? It wasn't an ideal life, spending seven days a week surrounded by the same four walls, with nothing to look at aside from little bottles of shampoo and tiny spray cans of deodorant. But at least it was theirs. No one could fire them. Jeremy admired the man's pride in his work and his store—and his daughter, or granddaughter, working with him, showing the same dedication to perfection.

The Korean man stepped down and put his duster handle first into his back pocket. "No food," he said, pointing to the bag Jeremy was holding.

"What?" Jeremy asked.

The teenage girl leaned around the meat slicer she was cleaning. "You can't bring outside food into the store," she said.

"It's just a basket of strawberries," Jeremy said.

"No food," the man said.

"I'll only be a minute," Jeremy said to him.

The man seemed not to understand. "No food," he said, as if they were the only two English words he knew.

"What am I supposed to do with it?" Jeremy asked.

"No food," the man said, nodding his head in agreement with himself.

"You can't stay in the store with outside food," the girl said.

The man with the bushy mustache remained at the window, looking in. Jeremy wasn't ready to face him.

"Here," Jeremy said, taking the basket out of the bag and handing it to the Korean man.

The man took the basket. He looked confused.

"You can have them," Jeremy said. "Put them in the salad bar. Sell them. I don't care."

The man studied the monstrous red-seeded specimens before him. The girl said something in Korean, presumably translating Jeremy's offer, and the man laughed. He spoke to her for a few seconds. Jeremy didn't like not understanding what people were saying.

"He doesn't want them," she told Jeremy.

"They're very good strawberries," Jeremy said.

"Keep them," the girl said.

"These strawberries are imported," Jeremy said, defensive. "You can't find them just anywhere, you know."

"We don't want them," she said.

"People are killing each other for strawberries like these,"

Jeremy said. "Just look at them. They're so big... please, take them."

"We don't want them," she said again.

"Neither do I."

"Sorry," she said.

Jeremy put the basket back into the white bag with King Strawberry its the side.

The man yelled something else in Korean.

"You can't have a bag in the store," the girl said.

"What?" Jeremy asked.

"Your bag, you can't have it in the store."

"Are you serious?"

"Yes."

"Why not?" Jeremy asked.

The man spoke again to her.

"Shoplifters," she translated.

"I'm not going to steal anything," Jeremy said.

"No bag!" the man yelled.

"You mean to tell me if I don't give you this bag I have to leave the store?"

"It's nothing personal," she said. "Just store policy."

"I don't want the bag," Jeremy said. "I only need it to carry the strawberries."

"Sorry," she said, "but policy is policy."

The man spoke rapidly to the girl.

"You'd better give me that bag," she said.

"This is no way to treat your customers," Jeremy said, giving her the bag and holding the basket of strawberries with his bare hand.

"It's policy," she said, apologetic but resigned to the inescapable way of things.

Jeremy didn't want anything from the grocery, but needed

to buy some time. He was hoping a plan of action would come to him if he stalled long enough. The man with the bushy mustache was waiting for him outside. Jeremy placed the basket of strawberries on the small table between the food bars and took a clear container. The grocery's proprietor made no effort to disguise his distrust of Jeremy, and watched him from just a few feet away.

Jeremy began with the salad bar. Come to think of it, he was hungry. The lettuce was green and fresh. Maybe a healthy meal would do him good. The tuna salad looked interesting, with chunks of celery and slivers of onion, but Jeremy had reservations about eating mayonnaise that had been sitting out all day. He took six cherry tomatoes, slices of cucumber, egg whites, croutons, bacon bits, green peppers, and topped it off with a heaping spoonful of Ranch dressing. The girl at the register wrapped the salad with a red rubber band, and was about to weigh it, but Jeremy stopped her. He wasn't done. The man with the bushy mustache had not tired yet, was still outside, and Jeremy needed more time. She could ring him up after he got some hot food. Man couldn't live on salad alone.

Condensation from the steaming food of the hot bar left the glass sneeze-guard dripping water. Jeremy got another plastic container. He took a chicken leg. And some fried rice. The lo mein noodles made his stomach growl—three helpings. The man with the bushy mustache hadn't moved. A spare rib, no, two. Meatballs with tomato sauce. They were small, so he grabbed four. That was a meal's worth of food. But the mysterious mustache man was still waiting, and Jeremy hadn't figured a way out, so he scooped sesame chicken with broccoli and deep-fried mushrooms and green beans. The container was filled to the very top and was heavy. Jeremy took a spoonful of sausage and peppers and a dinner roll and closed the plastic cover.

At the counter the girl needed both hands and was straining to wrap the food with a red rubber band.

"Is that all?" she asked.

Jeremy saw that the man with the bushy mustache was still outside, and thought about getting some soup to delay the inevitable, but worried that he was already spending too much money on lunch. "Yes, thank you," he said.

She placed the cold salad on the scale and pressed a button: .78 of a pound came to $2.80. Not too bad, Jeremy thought. The container of hot food made the delicate scale squeak. The green digital readout told him that he had purchased 2.7 pounds of food—he owed $11.48 plus the $2.80. His bill came to more than fifteen dollars, with tax.

"I can't afford that," Jeremy said.

"But you took all the food," the girl said.

"I know. I'm sorry."

"What am I supposed to do with the food?" the girl asked.

The Korean shopkeeper said something to her and she answered. He yelled. Jeremy was no linguist, but was sure the man had cursed him.

"You have to pay," the girl said to Jeremy.

"I can't pay."

The man walked over to the counter. He was older than Jeremy initially guessed. His frown highlighted the wrinkles on his face most unpleasantly. He picked up the container of hot food Jeremy had compiled and standing right in front of Jeremy screamed at him in Korean. The girl translated, her quiet voice just barely making itself heard above his ranting.

"You are a disgrace," the girl said. "It is people like you

who make this city a terrible place to live." She paused. "You're like all of them, wanting something for nothing. Have you no shame? Don't ever come back to my store. I don't ever want to see you here again."

She seemed to Jeremy to be interpreting the old man's words with care, perhaps softening them without changing their basic message.

"I'm sorry," Jeremy said to the man.

The man put the container back on the counter, but in his agitated state was careless, and it fell to the floor, despite its well-placed rubber band exploding forth projectiles of chicken and ribs and rice and breaded mushrooms. A solitary flying meatball splattered tomato sauce onto the man's pristine white apron.

Jeremy didn't know what to do.

The Korean man did. He reached behind the counter, by a whole chicken the girl had been slicing, and grabbed the long serving fork. Each of its two sharp prongs was three inches long. He held the fork up and yelled at Jeremy and the girl.

"Papa, no!" she shouted.

But he didn't listen, and pressed up close to Jeremy, sticking the fork against Jeremy's neck. Jeremy's hands were at his sides. He didn't think he was quick enough to disarm the man. The fork's prongs dug without breaking skin into the flesh below his Adam's apple, but the man didn't follow through, didn't plunge the utensil with bad intentions. He just held it there and yelled in words that no one understood. The girl had run out of the shop, but Jeremy couldn't see where she had gone. He was struggling to stay perfectly still, and didn't dare turn his head—he didn't know how long he stood there.

The man kept screaming, and Jeremy remained motionless. He hadn't imagined that destiny would see fit to end his life in such humiliating fashion. Then the girl came running back into the store.

"Put down the fork," a male voice said. "This is the police."

The girl translated into Korean.

The Korean man loosened his grip on Jeremy, lowered the hand holding the deadly fork, and an ugly shock of self-recognition came over him. He looked around his store, at the spilled food, at his own dirty apron, at the serving fork he had used to attack another human being, and began to sob, softly, at first. He sat down right there on the waxed tile and covered his eyes with his open hands.

"You all right?" the cop asked Jeremy.

"Yes," Jeremy said.

The police officer was tall and strong, with broad shoulders and light freckles on his cheeks. "We can book him on assault," he said to Jeremy, nodding to the old man still sitting on the floor crying. The girl was kneeling at the front of the store, picking up the food.

"No," Jeremy said. "I don't want to press charges."

"This man attacked you," the cop said. "He could've caused you serious bodily harm, even killed you. I've seen stranger things."

"I know," Jeremy said. "I won't press charges."

"What if he attacks someone else? Even kills them? It'll be on your conscience," the cop said.

"He won't attack anyone," Jeremy said.

"How do you know?" the cop asked.

"Because," Jeremy said, taking his basket of strawberries and heading toward the exit, "this was my fault. It had nothing to do with him at all."

The cop didn't stop him. Jeremy walked outside. He looked around for the man with the bushy mustache, ready to accept his fate, whatever it might be. He'd had enough. He didn't want to fight, couldn't bear the craziness any longer. But the man with the bushy mustache was not in sight. The police and the commotion must have scared him off.

Jeremy tossed the basket of strawberries into an orange, metal trashcan and went home. His stomach still gnawed at him, but Jeremy wasn't hungry.

Chapter 8

Jeremy couldn't afford a present for his mother's birthday, and had arrived already at his brother's building when he realized that he'd forgotten even to buy her a card. He didn't see the point of celebrating birthdays anyway. Staying alive one more year was no great accomplishment. It was just another excuse to eat cake. The trees outside the building were naked—their leaves had been gone for some time now. It was the middle of November but except for a lack of snow the city had the look of winter. Twinkling Christmas lights adorned doorways and windows of neighboring buildings. Such insipid displays were not permitted at Tranquil Manor.

Jeremy's brother, Marc, older by six years, lived on the East Side of Manhattan in a building overlooking the river. There were only four apartments per floor in the forty stories of Tranquil Manor, and the elevator operator didn't need to be told by guests the number of the apartment they were visiting—he knew all the residents by name, and if they were expecting visitors, he knew that as well. A Muzak rendition of Nirvana's *Territorial Pissings* filtered sweetly through speakers in the elevator ceiling and a red velvet cushioned seat, long enough for two people but wide enough for none, was at the back of the elevator. Jeremy sat. He knew that some people thought success came down to this: sitting on the elevator, without having to tell the operator what button to press. It was to them a true sign of achievement, to live in this building. And it wasn't just a matter of money, though the building was known for the wealth of its tenants. There were more expensive buildings in the city, and buying a private home in Great Neck or Scarsdale could run more. What they liked most about Tranquil Manor was the prestige and security associated with living there.

Everyone living in the building was a person of substance. The board of owners interviewed all prospective residents, did a background check in addition to the usual credit check, and required references from employers, previous landlords, and neighbors. It administered a psychological profile and social intelligence exam that had been written up in *Live, New York* magazine for its accuracy and thoroughness. There was no risk of being accosted by overfriendly neighbors, no knock on the door late at night from the precocious kid down the hall hocking cookies for her girl scout troop, no petitions posted in the lobby, nothing unexpected to interfere with a productive and busy life. People lived in this building safe from the breakdown of civilization taking place on the outside. Using only an elevator for transportation they could swim in the pool, play racquetball and basketball, work out, do light grocery shopping, get a haircut, visit the masseuse, or have a dress altered. Tranquil Manor, which Jeremy visited once or twice a year, when he was invited, made him want more than ever to discover his destiny, to do or be something that these people in their ivory tower couldn't buy.

Grooved fabric, a sort of platinum corduroy, covered the walls in Marc's home. Jeremy's sister-in-law had made it clear on his first visit to their apartment that the material was not to be touched by human hands. Skin's natural oils damaged it. Windows made up the living room's perimeter on two sides. A black leather L-shaped couch hugged the walls below the windows, and by pressing the button hidden behind a cushion one could lower tinted screens to block out the sun for afternoon naps. Not that Marc was the kind to take afternoon naps. He was so full of energy he seemed to not need sleep at all. Marc was taller than Jeremy, with darker hair and the same brown, almost black eyes. He had a fit, athletic build, from years of swimming and, more recently, racquetball.

There was a tradition in Jeremy's family that used to make him cringe in anticipation. Once a year the whole family sat in something like a circle, whenever something resembling the whole family managed to be in the same place, and one by one announced to the rest of the family what two of the year's events or accomplishments each of them was most proud or pleased about. In previous years Jeremy had faked excitement about his small raise at work, and buying a new futon, and the time he bowled a 221. The ritual, which was his mother's idea—she seemed to be the only one interested in keeping it alive, but that was enough—usually made Jeremy feel inadequate. He knew that the highlights of his life were petty and unworthy of announcement. His brother would never resort to bragging about a bowling score. But this time Jeremy was looking forward to letting the family know what an eventful year he'd had.

Jeremy's stepfather, Roddy, married to his mother for eight years now, was proud of losing six pounds, though his belly protruded the same as it always had, like a torpedo. But he was more proud of his jeans factory. This year he'd produced more jeans than he had in any year since 1981. The jeans produced in his factory were at one time the pinnacle of fashion. His company was the first to stitch designs on the back pockets of jeans, and he'd made millions of dollars before larger corporations latched onto his idea and took over the market. Fashions changed, but Roddy would not, and when dark blue jeans with stitched designs on the back pockets were no longer in demand, he continued to make them. "They'll come back," he said. "Everything does." He maintained copyrights on two hundred and sixteen stitch designs for that very reason.

At seventy-five he continued to go to the factory every day, and he and his three employees made jeans with the same equipment he had used back when people actually wanted to buy his product. He paid his employees and spent all of his days on the phone trying to sell his jeans to retailers, but no one was buying. There was simply no longer a market for his work. But he kept making jeans, and had to rent warehouse space near his upstate factory to store the hundreds of boxes of jeans nobody wanted. One of his employees brought a box or two of the jeans each week to the flea market, but no one there wanted any either. If any of this bothered him, Roddy didn't let on. What mattered was that this year he had made more jeans than in any since 1981. How much money he lost each year making the jeans and paying his staff nobody knew. It was a subject not to be broached in the presence of Jeremy's mother.

She was just happy to be with the whole family, and listed this birthday party as one of her highlights. One didn't turn sixty every day. But Marc's new charity, which he had formed with some business associates early in the year, was the source of her greatest pride. The buildings they renovated, the meal delivery programs they financed, were all she could talk about. Because of her son illiterate adults were learning to read, hungry children were being fed, people on the streets would have coats and a fighting chance against the coming winter. Friends she hadn't spoken to in months or years called her after reading about Marc's philanthropic group, Chipping In. All the local papers had taken notice of his new endeavor, and people who had once been indifferent to her now treated his mother like a minor celebrity.

Marc didn't finance the charity himself. His specialty was getting people to give him money, or whatever else he wanted, and to leave them believing that it was what they had wanted to do. Marc was a salesman. At seventeen he'd bought his first car, given it a paint job, and sold it for twice what he'd paid. He bought another car that same month with the money from the first one, tinted the windows and replaced the radio, and sold it a week later for a profit of $1,200. Over the next four years Marc bought and sold thirty-two cars. He paid his way through City College without ever holding a regular job. By the time he graduated with a business degree Marc had $15,000 to invest. He couldn't seem to make a wrong choice, and bought stocks on hunches and feelings, doubling his money in just a few weeks. He became a stockbroker, and was written up in *Money Journal* after his second year out of school, when he made his first million: *Marc Keller could sell water balloons to a drowning porcupine.* At thirty-three Marc gave up selling stocks and became a freelance consultant. When a company had to sell something, when a merger or acquisition needed approval from shareholders, anything that had huge sums of money resting on the outcome and required his subtle art of persuasion, Marc was brought in.

Marc didn't like to brag about his accomplishments, wasn't interested in publicity for his own sake, but was proud of Chipping In. The highlight of his year was of a personal nature, though—it was his new Porsche. He bought it to reward himself for helping the poor and disenfranchised. "Everyone should own a Porsche at least once before they die," he told Jeremy. It was one of the true worldly pleasures. Marc pulled a picture of it from his wallet. It was a beautiful car, with a black paint job and four big wheels and a sunroof. There was something about the power of this machine, the feel of its engine when he stepped on the gas, that purified its driver. "If you work hard," he said to his brother, "you could have one of these some day."

Their mother gazed at Marc with proud eyes before asking Herbert, her cousin, the retired podiatrist, to tell them his highlights. Herbert was sixty-eight, and told them that he was past the point of having highlights of his own. He lived for his grandchildren. His granddaughter in Chicago had made the honor roll in school, and his grandson was the leading scorer in the junior basketball league. Herbert could talk about his grandson for hours, but it always came down to shoe size. His grandson wore a size 11, tremendous for a nine-year-old. He was going to be tall. Maybe big enough for the NBA. Definitely a college prospect. He had feet like a puppy, a German Shepherd, Herbert said. You could tell by his feet that he had a lot of growing in him.

"What about you, Dear?" Jeremy's mother asked. "Anything exciting this year?"

Jeremy told them first that he'd met a woman, which surprised everyone.

What woman? Was it serious?

Her name was Brooke, and yes it was serious. She was kind and compassionate. Smart too. And beautiful. Her smile really lit up a room. It wouldn't surprise him if one day in the not-too-distant future she became Mrs. Jeremy Keller.

His mother interrupted him, saying that she wanted to change one of her highlights—could she replace her birthday with this wonderful news of her son's upcoming marriage?

Of course she could, Marc decided. It was her game, her birthday.

"That isn't all," Jeremy said, feeling hot as his cheeks flushed. "Something even bigger happened this year." He paused, to build suspense and drama.

"Well, what is it?" his mother asked. "What's bigger than falling in love?"

Jeremy put his hands out, palms down, seeking silence. He looked around, as if to be sure that no one was listening in, and said, "I'm being followed."

Herbert laughed first, and hardest. Tears streamed down his face and he nearly fell off the end of the leather couch. He was joined in his laughter by Jeremy's mother and her husband, and by Marc and his wife. Herbert stopped laughing long enough to congratulate Jeremy on his sense of humor. Jeremy was quite the cut-up. Being followed. Imagine. And what delivery, what timing. He hadn't even smiled as he'd said it: "I'm being followed." Just like that. He was a straight man in the tradition of May or Newhart. Had he considered a career in comedy?

"No, really, I'm serious. I'm being followed," Jeremy said.

Herbert had almost stopped laughing when these words were spoken. But Jeremy's insistent sincerity was too much, and Herbert did fall off of the couch this time. It was several minutes before he had calmed down enough to again thank Jeremy for his comedic talents.

Jeremy didn't know what he could say that would convince them. Was it so outrageous, so implausible, his being followed? They had accepted without question his relationship with Brooke, which was a fabrication. But he was being followed as sure as they were sitting there, and that they refused to believe. He laughed, like he was in on the joke and not the butt of it, and walked out of the room.

The family room was down the hall from the living room. A long red couch faced the big screen television mounted on the wall. Shelves lined the room, with all kinds of books about business, and selling, and history, and psychology. Some of the authors' names were familiar to Jeremy from his college days, but he didn't see anything he'd actually read. Jeremy's nephew, Drew, sat at a desk at the other end of the room playing a game on the computer. He was ten, and reminded Jeremy in all ways of Marc. Drew had his father's energy, the same agreeable, easy way of talking.

He was playing Subterranean Explorer, a first-person-point-of-view adventure game. The computer screen displayed in graphic detail only what the explorer saw, and he saw everything from behind the barrel of a gun, which he was compelled to use every few seconds, as mutated frogs and angry rats as big as ponies tried to make a meal out of him. Drew shot a frog, splattering red and green against a wall.

"You have to watch out for the frogs, Uncle Jeremy. They

can whip you with their tongues. It's much cooler when you have a shotgun," Drew told him. "But I haven't found one yet—whoa!" A rat lunged but was cut down by two quick shots. It lay on the ground, its tail still moving. Drew shot it again and it was still. "The rats don't die as easy as the frogs, unless you have a shotgun."

"Where are you?" Jeremy asked.

"The post-apocalyptic caverns are the abandoned remains of the New York subway," Drew said.

"Where'd you learn that word, 'post-apocalyptic?'"

"It says it on the box," Drew said.

"Why are they abandoned?" Jeremy asked.

Drew shot another frog. "Radiation. That's why the frogs are so big. And the rats. The worst ones are the people. They're all deformed from the radiation and they shoot back. But once I get a shotgun I can handle them. You have to get through the first level, kill the frogs and the rats. The second level has giant cockroaches. Then you get to the people."

"Why are you underground in the first place?" Jeremy asked.

"I don't know."

"Are you looking for treasure?" Jeremy asked.

"No," Drew said.

"Is there a cure for radiation at the end?"

"No."

"Are you rescuing a princess?"

"No."

"Why are you shooting all the frogs and rats, then?"

"Because that's the game," Drew said.

"Is there a point?" Jeremy asked.

"There is."

"What is it?"

"You have to kill all the frogs and the rats," Drew said.

"Why?"

"To get to the cockroaches. When you shoot them they screech and flip over and their legs wave around."

"And after that?"

"Then you get to fight the people," Drew said.

"And after you finish fighting the people, what happens?"

"I don't know," Drew said. "I haven't gotten that far. My friend has the game, but he hasn't gotten past the people either. I don't think you can."

"You have any other games?" Jeremy asked.

"On top of the desk, in the black case."

There was NFL Football, NBA Basketball, Home Run Baseball, NHL Hockey, Pro Ring Boxing, King of the Slopes Skiing, PGA Golf, African Safari, Sea Battle, Stealth Fighter, No-Fly Zone, Crash 'Em Derby, Wall Street Warrior, Monopoly, Invasive Surgery, Punitive Damages, Downtown Riot, The Guinness Book of World Records Encyclopedia, and three hand-to-hand martial-arts combat games—Rooftop Rage, Planet Pain, and Streets of Honor.

"Can I look at this?" Jeremy asked, handing him the Guinness Book CD.

"Sure," Drew said. "Let me save my game. Do you want to sit down?"

"No," Jeremy said. "You'd better stay. I don't know how to use this thing."

"What do you want to see?"

"Can we see the man who sleeps on the bed of nails?"

"That won't be in there," Drew said.

"Sure it will," Jeremy said. "It was in the actual museum I went to when I was a kid."

"It won't be here," Drew said.

"Why not?" Jeremy asked.

"Because of lawyers. My dad said that they were worried about being sued, so they took out dangerous things like climbing buildings and stuff. He said they were worried that it might give kids the wrong idea."

"Check anyway."

Drew typed in *nails* but only got the records for the people with the longest fingernails and toenails, accompanied by visuals of twisting and twirling nails at the ends of fingers and toes. "I told you," he said. "We can't have kids thinking it's OK to lie on a bed of nails, because of the lawyers."

"But what about your underground game? Won't that make kids like you want to shoot frogs and rats and deformed people?"

"That's different, Uncle Jeremy. That isn't real."

Jeremy couldn't disagree, and returned to the living room to find his stepfather and Marc in mid-argument. They never saw eye-to-eye on anything.

"He deserves whatever he gets," Roddy said. "They should lock him away and the victims' families should be allowed to mail bombs to his jail cell. The Unabomber—what kind of a name is that, anyway? If I were in charge I would appoint someone to punch him in the face. All we need in this country is to punch more people in the face. I know that look. You don't think it would stop crime, but it would. What we need are real penalties. Like, every hour, on the hour, for the rest of his life, someone should punch him in the face. In the middle of the night they should wake him up and punch him in the face. By the time he's fallen asleep again it's time for another punch. Maybe televise it. Kids would think twice about hurting someone if they knew they could be sentenced to a lifetime of being punched in the face. People used to fear the law. Sending bombs to someone's house. This kind of thing didn't used to happen."

"I'm only saying that it couldn't have been easy on his family, that's all," Marc said.

"Nonsense," Roddy said. "The man was killing people. They turned him in. What could be easier?"

"That was family they handed over to the FBI, not some stranger," Marc said.

"So?" Roddy asked.

"So," Marc said, "what if Mom were killing people and—"

"Your mother is not killing people, and she isn't writing a manifesto either," Roddy said.

"I know she isn't," Marc said. "I'm just saying suppose she was, and you found out, would you turn her in?"

"That's silly. Gwen could never kill anyone," Roddy said. "She has to call me into the bathroom to squash a spider."

"Yes, but suppose, for the sake of argument, that she could," Marc said.

"Which, squash a spider or write a manifesto?"

"Come on, Roddy. Suppose your wife killed someone. What if you saw her picture on *America's Most Wanted?* Would you call them up?"

"That depends," Roddy said.

"On what?" Marc asked.

"On the size of the reward."

Chapter 9

December's rent was due the first of the month. Jeremy was supposed to slip a check in the mail slot at his building's management office, five blocks away, but had verified his account balance at an ATM, and knew that writing a check for rent would be a gesture with no more than symbolic value. It would at best mean only that he had tried to pay his rent. In the end, when the check bounced, it would cost him fees he couldn't afford to pay. He didn't bother wasting the bank's time, and took pains to avoid seeing Mr. Valkof, knowing that the management company would soon send him to collect the past due rent.

Jeremy resolved to make a real effort to find a job, and was ashamed at his prior refusal to take this search more seriously. So what if he had wasted seven years and not found his destiny via the mailroom of a toy company? Most people spent lifetimes in similar pursuits. He would have to be careful not to become a snob of destiny, looking down on people just because their lives were ordinary. Feeling superior to regular hard work was a perversion of the values imparted to him by his father. Besides, at the moment his finances required a more egalitarian perspective.

Advertisements for jobs in the paper demanded degrees and experience Jeremy didn't have, his résumé and letters went unanswered, and on Tuesday of the first week of December he finally visited Job Bank Connection, a company in midtown specializing in career placement. The woman who interviewed him, Ms. Hirsch, had a wrinkled face and bags under her eyes. Her flat hair was closest to a shade of purple that Jeremy was certain did not exist in the natural world. She wore a floral-print blouse with a purple background. The purples matched too closely to be coincidental. Jeremy wanted to ask her whether the hair had inspired the purchase of the blouse, or the blouse the color of the hair.

"Thank you for choosing Job Bank Connection," Ms. Hirsch said, "the Fort Knox of career services." Her desk was cluttered with folders and résumés. There was a picture in a silver frame of she and her family, a husband and two grown sons, both boys in their twenties. She was the only one with purple hair.

"That's a nice blouse," Jeremy said. "I don't think I've ever seen that color purple before."

She ignored him and looked over his job application, her narrow glasses sliding down to the tip of her nose. "I see here you worked for seven years at the same company... Dubasky and Cohen. What did you do there?"

"I performed a variety of functions," Jeremy said.

"It says here you worked in the mailroom."

"Yes, but I did more than deliver mail. Much more."

"Such as..."

"Well, I contributed proposals to the Promotions Department," Jeremy said.

"Really? That's good. Do you have copies of any of the completed projects?" she asked.

"They didn't exactly use any of them," Jeremy said. "Say, if I went to the store and wanted to buy a blouse like yours, what color would I ask for?"

"What did you do besides deliver mail, not counting the marketing ideas they didn't use?" Ms. Hirsch asked, fidgeting with a paper clip.

"Well, like my application says, I delivered mail. But I also managed the supply cabinet, and did some packaging."

"Oh, you do packaging for toys? That's good. What design programs do you know?"

"I don't know any," Jeremy said. "Most of the packaging I did was around the holidays. You know, wrapping gifts from executives to other executives. Sometimes I had to pack a toy sample and send it to a retailer. The trick is to use plenty of bubble wrap."

"So you didn't do packaging. You just packed and wrapped boxes. Was that all?" she asked.

"And I kept up the supply cabinet."

"Anything else?" she asked.

"You make it sound like that isn't a lot."

"It's not that, Mr. Keller," Ms. Hirsch said. "I'm trying to determine what careers you might be qualified for. Is there someone I can call at Dubasky and Cohen for a reference?"

Jeremy didn't know what they might say about him, so he lied. "My supervisor just left as well. I don't know where to reach him."

"Do you have any computer skills?" she asked.

"No, not really," Jeremy said. "But I've been meaning to learn."

"It says here you scored fifteen words per minute on the

typing test."

"Is that good?"

"It's a little low for most receptionist positions," Ms. Hirsch said.

"Well, I wasn't really thinking of being a receptionist. Aren't there bigger opportunities for someone with my particular talents?"

"What exactly are your particular talents, Mr. Keller?"

He thought for a second. "I'm a hard worker."

"Mr. Keller, everyone is a hard worker. Or claims to be. What do you offer that they don't?"

"Imagination," he said.

"Imagination?" she asked.

"That's right," he said.

"Is that all?"

"Isn't imagination worth anything?" Jeremy asked.

"Not unless you're writing a book. I wouldn't mention the i-word on any interviews. People don't like someone who thinks too much. Look, I'll enter this information into our computer, check our listings, see if I can't find you something. But I'd keep looking in the papers if I was you."

"Thank you," he said, getting up to leave.

"By the way, Mr. Keller, the color is hyper-magenta. It's available in most drugstores. But I don't think dyeing your hair will help your chances of finding a job."

Alone on the subway platform waiting to go home, Jeremy felt the bleak reality of his occupational prospects. He'd always thought of himself as the independent, resourceful sort. He worked hard. He would say uncommonly hard. And he'd been over the years nothing if not loyal. But loyalty didn't count for much anymore. No one had told him it wouldn't last. There was no warning. Part of him wished he could go back to the way things were, to once again lead his mundane life and deliver mail. What were a few paper cuts and missed promotions compared to obsolescence at thirty years of age? But he understood that he couldn't go back even if he wanted to. He wasn't sure he wanted to—his desire to be more than he was would not be vanquished by minor setbacks. The greatest people in every society always overcame obstacles. It might even be said that they owed their greatness to those obstacles.

A growing rumbling and vibrations in the floor and the air made Jeremy anticipate his train, but it was an express, and didn't stop for him. The train rushing by blasted him with a shock of warm, stale wind, carrying with it the smell of urine. It was the city. It wasn't possible to get from point A to point B without being visited by some insult. Conflict with other people wasn't even necessary—the city was quite capable of committing its own impersonal offenses. It was enough to break some people. But Jeremy would remain committed to his idea of himself and the active pursuit of his destiny, even if it meant he had to take on the entire city to reach it.

Standing at the edge of the platform, on the dimpled, yellow warning track, Jeremy leaned to see down the train tunnel, staring in total concentration, as if he could will the train to appear. No train lights illuminated the distant darkness. A boy, maybe twelve years old, walked toward him. He looked lost; his innocent little eyes seemed to be seeking assurance from Jeremy that this was the right platform. Jeremy showed him a friendly smile. The boy was Hispanic and wore a bulging winter coat; its thick lining gave him the appearance of a comic book superhero, limited in range of motion by his own extreme muscularity. His right hand was in his coat pocket and he stopped a few feet from the edge of the platform and Jeremy. He looked around. No one else was on the platform.

"Hey," the boy asked, "what if I told you I got a gun?"

Jeremy was lost in his own thoughts. He knew he had been spoken to but didn't know what the boy had said. "I'm sorry. What was that?"

"What if I told you I got a gun?" The boy motioned with the hand in the coat pocket.

"Do you have a gun?" Jeremy asked.

"You think I'm frontin'? You callin' my bluff?" the boy asked.

"No. But how am I supposed to answer you? Telling me you have a gun and having a gun are two very different things," Jeremy said.

"I got one," the boy said, shifting his weight from one foot to the other.

"I think if you had a gun you would've shown it to me already. No one tells people they have a gun. Waving one around usually does the trick," Jeremy said.

"I do got a gun. Don't make me show it to you. What do you got to say to that?"

"I don't know," Jeremy said.

"Maybe you didn't hear me. I said I got a gun."

"I heard you. I just don't have anything to say."

"You think I won't shoot you?" the boy asked.

"I don't know what you'll do. You're the one with the gun," Jeremy said.

"That's right. You got any money?" the boy asked.

"Not really," Jeremy said.

"What does 'not really' mean?" the boy asked.

"Things have been tight lately. I lost my job, and my computer skills aren't what they should be."

"I don't care about your job."

"Have you ever been fired?"

"No—I'm the one asking the questions here. I'm the one with the gun," the boy said.

"You're the one with the gun," Jeremy agreed.

"Give me my money," the boy said.

"Maybe I should go back to school," Jeremy said. "I never should have quit. Do yourself a favor. Stay in school."

"You gotta have some money. Don't make me shoot you."

"Let me check," Jeremy said, searching his pockets. He handed the boy a quarter.

"A quarter? I tell you I got a gun and all you got is a quarter?"

"It's all I can spare," Jeremy said.

"Four hundred years of slavery and oppression and all you got for me is a quarter?"

"What does slavery have to do with it? You're not even black."

"I've been oppressed. I don't gotta be black," the boy said.

"We've all been oppressed," Jeremy said.

"You're not like me," the boy said. He was angry, but was careful not to raise his voice.

"Sorry," Jeremy said.

"Listen, I'm the one with the gun. I want more money."

"Do you have change of a five?" Jeremy asked.

"No."

"Fine," Jeremy said, and handed the boy five dollars.

The boy took the money with his left hand, the one not holding the gun. "I'm going now. If I catch you looking at me I'll shoot you. Count to a thousand."

"A thousand?" Jeremy asked.

"Yeah, a thousand."

"I will not count to a thousand," Jeremy said.

"I got a gun," the boy said.

"So you keep saying."

"I *will* shoot you," the boy said.

"Then shoot me," Jeremy said. "I gave you all my money, the guy who was following me hasn't shown his face in months, I don't know what was in that stupid envelope, and poor Claude slashed his wrists. My rent is late, I've been hiding from Mr. Valkof for a week, and Brooke doesn't know I'm alive. I was told today that I'm incapable of doing anything but sorting mail. I can take that. I can take all of it. But I will not count to a thousand. Do you understand me? I will not count to a thousand. I have a life to get on with, if you want to call it that, so if you're going to shoot me, please do it now."

"Forget a thousand," the boy said. "Count to a hundred."

"No," Jeremy said.

"Will you count to fifty?" the boy asked.

"I will count to twenty-five, and no higher."

"Count to twenty-five," the boy commanded.

"One, two, three, four…"

The boy ran to the exit at the end of the subway platform, the empty station briefly filled by the hard and clear echo of his rapid steps.

"Five, six, seven, eight, nine…"

The boy pushed the turnstile and dashed up the stairs, emerging from the damp underground into the sunlight reflecting brightly from the cars and buildings and asphalt of the city's surface.

The boy might easily have had a gun, might have killed him, and Jeremy thought that perhaps destiny was keeping him from harm's way for some purpose. A five-dollar bill was no great loss in the big picture—there were kids killing each other for less—and to Jeremy the boy's desperation justified the loss. His need for the money was even more acute than Jeremy's. This rationalization allowed him a moment of self-congratulation at the voluntary spirit of his coerced good deed, but didn't remove the ache of being without work, of not knowing what step to take next, of doubting his ability to be a useful part of the world around him.

Jeremy's belief in destiny didn't allow him to resent his former employer for his current financial situation. It was hard to hold them responsible for what he saw primarily as an act of fate. Not that Jeremy abdicated responsibility for his life. Fate and free will were not incompatible, and he saw no paradox in working to achieve what destiny promised. Dubasky and Cohen was merely an instrument in his search, and his no longer being with them certainly served some larger purpose. What it was he wasn't sure, but a part of him worried that fate had intervened specifically to protect him from some catastrophe that was going to befall the company.

He knew that this was probably his own overreaction or a misunderstanding of destiny. Fate rarely took a route as obvious as blowing up a building. But if he were right, and didn't warn them, the lost lives of hundreds of innocent people would be on his conscience. Almost two and a half months after losing his job, immediately following his interview at Job Bank Connection and being mugged by a twelve-year-old boy, in the spirit of compassion and without malice, he sent the Vice President of Promotions at Dubasky and Cohen the following handwritten letter:

Dear Mr. Foster,

I am writing about a matter of extreme importance. My name is Jeremy Keller, and I am a former employee from the mailroom (you will remember me from the marketing proposals I used to send you). Anyway, I was recently fired and it occurred to me that this might be a sign. Of what I don't know, but I think fate may have been protecting me from some horrible accident at Dubasky and Cohen. Maybe a fire, or a bomb. Perhaps you have a disgruntled employee with a collection of rifles at home. I could be wrong, and I hope I am, but anything is possible in today's world. I think you owe it to your employees and the other people in your building to keep an eye out for anything suspicious.

Sincerely,
Jeremy Keller

P.S. After reading this letter over it occurs to me that it could be misread as a threat. It is not.

Chapter 10

On Thursday morning in mid-December there was a knock on the door to Jeremy's apartment. He had just finished eating his breakfast, a peanut butter and jelly sandwich on white bread. As a child he had loved peanut butter and jelly, as most kids do, but his affection for it had diminished considerably after consuming in the week since his visit to Job Bank Connection twenty-six peanut butter and jelly sandwiches. Jeremy was silent, hoping that the person knocking would give up and go away.

Knock, knock, knock. From outside the door Mr. Valkof shouted, "Mr. Keller, are you in there? Please, Mr. Keller, open the door."

Jeremy had since the third of December managed not to see Mr. Valkof. It hadn't been easy. Mr. Valkof was always in the hallways changing a light bulb, or mopping the stairs, or picking up around the garbage cans fenced in outside the front of the building. It had been twice necessary for Jeremy to use his fire escape to go to Strawberry Dreams. In his caution he adopted the habit of watching television during the day with the sound turned off, in case Mr. Valkof was on his floor, and had found that daytime talk shows made as much sense, if not more, when muted. The people on these shows were actors even to themselves, trying to capture the essence of the victims they had been trained since birth to portray. The issues they yelled and screamed and cried about on the television differed depending on the show's theme, but they always cried and screamed and yelled in the same way. Captions identifying the shows' participants told enough of the story: *Thirteen-year-old mother is a pyromaniac* or *Cheated on his mistress with her sister*. Even without sound their lives on television diverted Jeremy from wallowing in his lack of anything important to do with his time. There is no one so low that can't be made to feel better by seeing someone lower.

Jeremy had avoided Mr. Valkof because he didn't want to lie to him, didn't want to tell him that he would run to the management office first thing in the morning, since until now it was not something he was prepared to do. But Jeremy had lined up employment to begin the next day, through an ad in the paper. The job didn't pay much, but not much under the table was better than the on-the-books not muches he wasn't being offered elsewhere. And the beauty of his new job was that it allowed him to continue to receive unemployment checks. He would go tomorrow to his building's management office and write them a post-dated rent check. They wouldn't like it, but would take what they could get. Jeremy had a long history of on-time payments, and eviction was an expensive and lengthy process.

When Jeremy opened the door he found Mr. Valkof pacing up and down the hallway. He walked with a trace of a waddle. His hands were clasped behind his back and he kept his eyes on the floor, not seeing Jeremy. Mr. Valkof nodded and shook his head as if he were silently rehearsing his lines for a play or, more likely, some unpleasant but unavoidable conversation. He turned on his heel and walked again toward Jeremy's door, finally looking up to see the cause of his worried expression.

"Mr. Keller," Mr. Valkof said, "I didn't think you were home."

"I was. I mean, I am," Jeremy said.

"You have put me in an awkward position, Mr. Keller. A very awkward position."

"I know," Jeremy said. "I'm sorry."

"This is my job, you understand. I don't do this for fun."

"I know, Mr. Valkof, but—"

"If I were mopping for the sheer joy of it then I wouldn't mind, you see. But this is my job, you understand."

"I appreciate that—" Jeremy started to say.

"I don't know if you do, Mr. Keller. The people who pay me and feed me and my wife are the people who you pay rent to. It's my job to make sure you pay them the money."

"I was going to talk to them tomorrow," Jeremy said. "I have a new—"

"This job is putting our daughter through college, you see. She wants to be a doctor," Mr. Valkof said. "But I guess I'll have to tell her she can't be a doctor now. She was going to be the first Valkof with a college diploma. But I can't keep my job if the tenants don't pay their rent."

"Mr. Valkof—"

"Don't worry about her," Mr. Valkof said. "There are some good technical schools here in New York. She's a smart girl. I'm sure she'll get financial aid to one of them. What's the name of that school, on the West Side? You know the one I mean, the one that teaches air condition repair?"

"She doesn't have to go to a technical school," Jeremy said.

"That, Mr. Keller, is up to you."

"I'm trying to tell you that I'm paying my rent tomorrow," Jeremy said. "I have a new job."

"What wonderful news. Congratulations," Mr. Valkof said.

"Thank you," Jeremy said. "And I'm sorry about making you come ask me for the rent."

"A new job. My daughter will be happy to hear it. She wants so to be a doctor, a pediatrician. And my wife, when she finds out that we don't have to live on the sidewalk, will be thrilled."

Jeremy knew he deserved this mockery. But he didn't want to remain on poor terms with Mr. Valkof; besides his ability to directly impact Jeremy's life through his role as the building's super, Mr. Valkof had always been kind and helpful. "Maybe I'll be in a position to help your daughter, when she finishes school. My new job is at a hospital." Jeremy's new job was not at a hospital.

All hint of Mr. Valkof's sarcasm vanished. "At a hospital? Thank you so much. You have no idea what this means to me. To my whole family. If you ever need anything you just let me know."

"Thank you," Jeremy said. When he shut the door on Mr. Valkof he closed one as well on his own pangs of guilt. Debt was never pleasant, but Jeremy's childhood memory of his father's credit card troubles made owing money especially distasteful to him.

There was again a knock on his door. Jeremy opened it, saying as he did, "Yes, Mr. Valkof, what can I do for you?"

Mr. Valkof was not outside the door. Two men were.

They both wore sport coats. The taller of the two, a black man with a shaved head, held out a badge. "Jeremy

Keller?" he asked.

"Yes," Jeremy answered.

"My name is Detective Jackson, NYPD. Can we come in?"

"What's the matter? It isn't my mother, or my brother?" Jeremy asked, fearing the worst.

"This isn't about any member of your family, Mr. Keller. We'd just like to have a word with you. May we come in?" Detective Jackson asked.

"What is this about?"

"It would be easier if we could come in and talk," Detective Jackson said.

"If it would be easier, I guess you can come in."

He stepped out of their way and closed the door after they'd entered his studio apartment.

Detective Jackson held a folded piece of paper. The other man, white and wearing glasses, with patches on the elbows of his jacket, surveyed Jeremy's apartment, but never said a word. He took a small spiral notebook and a well-chewed pencil out of the inside pocket of his sport coat.

"Do you know why we're here?" Detective Jackson asked.

Jeremy shook his head.

"Do you know anything about a letter to Dubasky and Cohen, mailed on December the seventh?" Detective Jackson asked.

"Is that what this is about?" Jeremy asked.

"So you admit to writing the letter?" Detective Jackson asked. The other man scribbled in his notebook.

"What is he writing?" Jeremy asked.

"Don't worry about him, Mr. Keller. You should be worrying about yourself. Please answer my question. Do you admit to writing a letter to Dubasky and Cohen?"

"I don't know about admitting. I did write a letter, though.

So?"

"So, Mr. Keller? So? Do you have any idea what the penalty is for threatening to plant a bomb in a building?" Detective Jackson asked.

"No," Jeremy said.

"Well, it's more time than you can handle, that much I can assure you," Detective Jackson said.

"Time?"

"Jail time," Detective Jackson said.

"Jail? For writing a letter?"

"Don't play dumb with me, Mr. Keller. There is at the moment no law against writing letters. It *is* a crime to blow up a building, however. It is also currently illegal to intentionally burn a building to the ground. It is equally unlawful to shoot down former colleagues in a fit of rage."

"I haven't done any of those things," Jeremy said.

"Not yet, you mean," Detective Jackson said.

"No, I wouldn't—"

Detective Jackson interrupted. "What were you going to do, come up with some sob story about how they teased you at work, how they were talking about you behind your back? Was that the plan, Mr. Keller? Say that the stress pushed you over the edge, then plead insanity, while the families of those dead men and women tried to put their lives back together?"

"I didn't have any plan."

"Don't lie to me, Keller. Who do you think you're talking to? I'm a detective. This is what I do for a living. You had a plan. You're the planning type," Detective Jackson said, pointing his finger.

"I wouldn't hurt anyone," Jeremy said.

"Save it. Your letter speaks for itself." Detective Jackson unfolded the paper he was holding and read from it. "These are your words, Mr. Keller: 'Maybe a fire, or a bomb. Perhaps you have a disgruntled employee with a collection of rifles at home. Anything is possible in today's world.' Sound familiar?"

"I wasn't talking about myself," Jeremy said.

"Do you own any rifles?" Detective Jackson asked.

"No. And my letter made it clear that I wasn't threatening anyone."

"Is that the story you're going to stick to?"

"It isn't a story. It's the truth."

"Maybe to you it is," Detective Jackson said.

"This is just a misunderstanding. I haven't done anything wrong. Nobody's been hurt. I didn't mean to cause any problems. Really, I didn't."

"Well you've caused plenty," Detective Jackson said.

"Look, I didn't break any laws."

"I'll be the judge of that."

"Am I being charged with a crime?"

"No. Technically speaking, you didn't break any laws. Technically speaking."

"In that case I would like you to leave my apartment," Jeremy said.

"I'll have my eye on you, Keller," Detective Jackson said.

"Yes, I'm sure you will. Could you please go now."

"Your kind makes me sick," Detective Jackson said, then turned to his partner. "Let's go."

Jeremy was relieved when they left. But before he had secured the chain there was again a knock at his door. Jeremy was worried that they had more questions for him, and looked through his peephole. It wasn't Detective Jackson and his silent, scribe of a partner.

It was, however, the man with the bushy black mustache.

Chapter 11

It was the man with the bushy black mustache.

He knocked again on Jeremy's door.

Jeremy stared through the peephole, indecision paralyzing him. His heart beat ever quicker.

"Jeremy," the man called from outside the closed door.

To Jeremy the man was a forgotten symbol from an unremembered dream—with a meaning no one could decipher. It had been so long since he'd shown himself. Jeremy had even begun to doubt the man's role as an instrument of destiny. And in its absence Jeremy had come to see the envelope for what it was, merely a hint—a catalyst—with no value of its own. He had ceased to think of the man or the contents of the envelope as being directly relevant to his life, a life that had of late been speeding by. Jeremy had until now been swept up by events and his own determined energy, without any idea of where he was heading. Everything had happened faster than thought's ability to keep up, and Jeremy felt that he had been reacting to his life instead of living it. But the man was there, right outside his door, concrete and real, and the waves of fear and wonder and joy Jeremy had felt when he first realized he was being followed returned to him, leaving in their wakes any glimmer of doubt. The man's appearance outside his door confirmed the proper course of Jeremy's decisions up to this point. He was now entering a more sensitive phase of the adventure, though, and would have to be cautious. This was it. Destiny, at last.

"Jeremy," the man said, even through the door his voice strong and clear.

Jeremy didn't answer.

"Jeremy, I need to talk to you."

Jeremy was silent.

"I know you're in there, Jeremy. I saw you open the door for your super, and I saw those men come to talk to you. They looked like cops. Are you in some kind of trouble with the police?"

Jeremy was afraid to speak. As long as he didn't acknowledge the man his fate remained undecided, his options open. Accepting the man would be committing himself to a destiny about which he knew nothing.

"I don't have all day, Jeremy," the man said. "Open the door."

It was a risk. Destiny was enigmatic. He didn't know whether the man was here to help him or if he was a foil to Jeremy's vague and lofty aspirations.

"I guess I was wrong about you," the man said. "I have a schedule to keep." He walked toward the stairs.

"Wait!" Jeremy shouted. Opportunity had knocked, and he couldn't live with himself if he did nothing, not after all he'd been through.

"Jeremy, open up. This is ridiculous. Two grown men talking through a door."

"I prefer to keep it closed."

"I'm not going to hurt you."

"I don't know that," Jeremy said.

"If I had wanted to do anything to you, wouldn't I have done it already? You know I had plenty of opportunities."

"What do you want with me?"

"I can't be screaming it out for the whole building to hear. Open this door or I'm going to have to leave."

"You were following *me*," Jeremy said. "I didn't ask for you. You're here at *my* door. I didn't come looking for you. You came looking for me."

"I did come looking for you, Jeremy. I did. And now I'm here. What am I supposed to do now?"

"I don't know."

"Why don't you just let me in?"

"I have a better idea. Why don't we meet at a neutral site, in public? I think I'd feel safer."

"A neutral site? Come on, there's no need for these melodramatic precautions. This isn't an espionage movie."

"And I'm not James Bond," Jeremy said. "I'm not followed all the time, either, and I say we meet at a neutral site, during the day, so there'll be plenty of witnesses."

"Fine," the man said. "Where?"

"I don't know. I've never done anything like this before."

"Anything like what?"

"All this sneaking around. Why don't you pick a place? You have more experience at this sort of thing."

"How about Washington Square Park," the man said. "It's near my office."

"You have an office?"

"Does that surprise you?"

"A little," Jeremy said.

"What do you think, all I do is follow people?"

"Well..."

"Look, this isn't something I do all the time, either. But you're a special case."

Jeremy couldn't help smiling at this. He *was* a special case. "Thank you," he said.

"Washington Square Park, the southeast corner," the man said. "When?"

"Tomorrow, at noon," Jeremy said. He wanted to slow things down, give himself a day to put this all in perspective. A day to bask in the knowledge that he had been right, that all his time waiting was not in vain. Tomorrow at high noon seemed an appropriate hour to learn his fate.

"Noon's no good," the man said. "I don't take lunch until one. How about a quarter after?"

"A quarter after one?" Jeremy asked. It wasn't as dramatic as high noon.

"A quarter after one," the man said, "tomorrow."

"I'll be there," Jeremy said.

Through the peephole Jeremy watched the man's form recede and disappear. He strained to hear footsteps descending the stairs.

The nights, the days too, he had spent in miserable self-loathing seemed far away—a universe away. The years of sleepless frustration, staring through the darkness at the ceiling, the recent weeks in front of the television in silent fascination at the degraded lives of strangers, the lifetime of bruises on his ego and his heart, all disappeared almost from memory when he saw the man outside his door, and did finally fade from even the recesses of his mind when the man had left. All things were possible now. He felt a new confidence, not the forced bravado he sometimes employed to combat his own weakness and self-doubt, but a genuine understanding of his importance. He felt the happiness that distinguishes knowing from believing. The mysterious man had visited him, and no one else.

Jeremy opened his door with caution, peeking around its edge and bracing it with both arms, leaning his weight to guard against forced entry. He didn't distrust the man with the bushy mustache, didn't really believe that he was still around and waiting for a chance to strike, but would not let a misjudgment doom his destiny before he'd had the opportunity to make it real. A door opened at the other end of the hallway.

It was his neighbor, a blonde woman with a crooked nose, older than he was by a few years. She was almost as tall as Jeremy. Her gray scarf and long black coat reflected the serious professionalism of her blue eyes. She was carrying narrow cardboard boxes, stacked a precarious six high, and with her free hand tried to lock her door behind her, in her hurry dropping the boxes. Two of them opened and dozens of greeting cards poured out. Jeremy didn't know her name, but then aside from Mr. Valkof he didn't know the name of anyone in the building. He was accustomed to living in anonymity and had never known any of his neighbors in any of the buildings in which he'd resided. They didn't bother him and he didn't bother them. A smile or a nod was the extent of his contact with the people who shared his address, and he'd liked it that way. Just a few months earlier he would have closed his door and pretended that he hadn't seen her.

Not getting involved was always the easiest path, and he'd

lived enough years in the city and read enough newspapers to know it was safest too. But he was nothing if not involved—with Claude, with Brooke, with the grieving parents in the hospital's waiting room, with the boy at the subway station. Life had a way of drawing him in. He no longer minded his own business because he was beginning to believe that everything was his business. Jeremy walked over and helped her pick up the cards and put them into the boxes.

"Hi," he said, and introduced himself.

Her name was Holly Day. It was OK to laugh, she said. She was sure her parents had laughed themselves when they'd named her. Holly didn't hold any anger toward them, though. She credited their choice in names for her artistic soul, her free spirit. She ran her own greeting card company, right out of her studio apartment. Happy Holly Day's Greetings, she called it. She hadn't started out in the card business. Actually, she was a poet. No, she wasn't published, but she got her Master of Fine Arts in poetry five years ago. Though with her name she knew she was destined from the beginning to a life of making greeting cards. Now she worked for herself, used her God-given talents to spread a little joy, to bring some hope and optimism to even the darkest corners of the human heart. To what higher purpose could she dedicate her gifts? There was nothing more important.

"I don't know much about poetry," Jeremy said. "But to me the main thing is that you found your destiny."

"Do you send a lot of cards?" she asked.

"I hardly ever send cards," Jeremy said.

"Take a look, anyway. These are Holly Day originals. I do the illustrations myself, too. Maybe you'll find something you like. It might be worth money one day."

Jeremy looked through the handful of cards that had spilled out of a box. He finally settled on this:

*your smile melts the winter's snow,
your voice scares the clouds away,
the sun shines and flowers grow
for you on Valentine's Day!*

On the cover of the card was a snowman with a broad smile, sketched in black ink. His icy fist held a bunch of daisies. Jeremy was no judge of literature, but liked the drawing of the simple snowman. He didn't want any of Holly's cards, really, but didn't want to insult her.

"For your girlfriend?" Holly asked.

"Yes," Jeremy said. Girlfriend sounded too inconsequential. He was thirty, an adult, about to embark on a crucial stage of his destiny, and didn't have even a girlfriend to share it with. Just a pretend girlfriend. "Actually, she'll be my fiancée soon. I'm on my way to see her now."

"That's wonderful," Holly said. "Congratulations."

"How about you?" Jeremy asked.

"Oh," Holly said, "I'm not with anyone."

"Sorry to hear that," Jeremy said.

"Don't be. I'm happy. My art is my first love. The truest love of all. Any man would have to share me with the Muse. I haven't found one yet who could. I don't mean to go on so," Holly said, her eyes nearly transparent, "but most people don't know what it's like to believe in something this passionately."

"I think I know what you mean."

"I don't think you could," she said.

"Well—"

"Since I was a little girl I've had words in my head. I'd go to sleep with the words and when I'd wake up they'd still be there. Do you know what that's like?"

"I suppose not," he said.

"It isn't easy."

"Is that why you write cards?"

"I don't just write cards," Holly said. "I'm making a statement. I put a little of myself into every poem, into each drawing."

"What's this one saying?" Jeremy asked, genuinely curious, holding up the cover of the snowman with the flowers.

"That everything will be all right," she said. "That even in the cold ice of our hearts we can find some beauty, that the good in us can overcome the evil, that humanity's better days are still ahead."

"I thought it was about a girl with a pretty smile," Jeremy said.

"You're right. You don't know anything about poetry."

Chapter 12

Yes.

She'd said yes.

Jeremy had asked out Brooke and she'd said yes. Actually, she'd said no, but she'd meant yes. She would go out with him, and she would do it tonight.

Less than an hour after the man with the bushy mustache had left his door, Jeremy just walked into Strawberry Dreams, like he had every day for the last three months, and surprised himself by asking, "Brooke, do you have plans for dinner?" After he'd said the words he was struck by how easy they were to say, seven simple words that until today he was unable to form. But the confidence of knowing he was a special case carried him along. He would not be like Holly, clinging to an insignificant destiny at all costs. He would not be alone.

Brooke's response was even simpler than Jeremy's question: "No." She didn't have plans for dinner, and would be happy to go out with him. No was a beautiful answer when paired with the right question. The purest of words—it cut through all possibility of misunderstanding. Her no still echoed in his ears. The world would be a better place if only more people mastered the use of yes and no. It really all came down to yes and no. Jeremy was a yes person. He'd said yes to life, had said it in seven words, and wouldn't say no again.

At nine Jeremy was supposed to meet Brooke at Towering Cuisine, a restaurant on the West Side known more than anything for the height of its food. The head chef had won awards for his ability to sculpt and shape dishes. Brooke told Jeremy that she'd always wanted to go there—she'd heard the Leaning Tower of Pizza was to die for—and he called for dinner reservations as soon as he left Strawberry Dreams. A table for two. No need to ask for the no smoking section since New York City had outlawed smoking in restaurants and most public places.

Jeremy took a close shave and ironed his khaki slacks and his button-down evergreen shirt. Several minutes of thought were required to select the right cologne. He had twenty bottles, all gifts he'd received over the years. Jeremy did not normally wear any, but guessed that Brooke would appreciate the effort. The problem was choosing. All of the bottles, the translucent blues and browns and solid blacks, were covered with dust. Some of the colognes were probably no longer available in stores, and Jeremy wondered if any in his collection might be worth money, maybe as antiques. Worried that he might pick an outdated scent, he finally chose the solid black bottle of Warrior in the back row, remembering a recent ad of a chiseled and glistening man, punching a heavy bag and shooting a bow and arrow, being greeted by a beautiful woman in an evening gown.

She'd handed the pretty pugilist a towel to wipe the sweat from his neck and face. Optimistic, Jeremy didn't anticipate archery or hand-to-hand combat on his date with Brooke, but chose the Warrior anyway, to guard against smelling old-fashioned.

Towering Cuisine was down a flight of stairs, two large rooms each seeming larger due to a shared wall mirrored on both sides. Jeremy was fifteen minutes early—it was 8:45. He checked in with the hostess, a half-black, half-Asian woman with bright red fingernails. Her white blouse was tucked into her black miniskirt. "Your table is waiting, Mr. Keller." It was the first time in a long while anyone had called him Mr. Keller without using the formal salutation as an ironic weapon, to convey something other than the respect it implied. There was nothing but courtesy from the hostess, and Jeremy decided that he liked this restaurant.

Brooke smiled at Jeremy when she arrived, just a few minutes past nine. He'd never seen her without her floppy hat with its strawberry pattern. She was truly beautiful. Her hair was wavier than he'd ever seen it, cascading into delicate curls and nearly reaching the small of her back. She wasn't wearing makeup or nail polish, at least none that announced itself, and she was all the more beautiful for her natural look. Brooke had on pleated burgundy pants and a black form-fitting velvet top—it might have only been something resembling velvet, but the form-fitting part was what got Jeremy's attention. Even with her two-inch heels she was quite a bit shorter than he was. They were seated right away.

Brooke liked to talk. Not just about herself, mind you, but it *was* their first date, and even though she felt that she knew him from his visits to Strawberry Dreams, she really didn't know anything about him. And he knew nothing about her. Where to begin? She wasn't going to work at Strawberry Dreams forever, though she liked her job—good benefits, flexible hours, and, most of all, she loved the free strawberries. But she had bigger plans. Brooke was attending school, one night a week at New York University. She was studying psychology, a year away from getting her master's. Abnormal psych intrigued her. Did Jeremy have any idea of the complexities of the human mind? No? Well, she assured him that it was very interesting stuff. Not that she had tunnel vision only for her career. A family was on the agenda too. Five kids. She was an only child, and she wanted plenty of children, so they would always have each other. It was lonely growing up without a sister. Not that she wanted kids any time soon. She was only twenty-four, and there was plenty of time. First she had to finish school. And if she decided to go for her doctorate it would be years before she was ready.

Jeremy gazed into the emerald sea of her not-green eyes. She was what he needed, he thought. So human, so grounded in the happy possibilities of a normal life. He hoped his destiny wouldn't exclude the bliss of being with her.

"What do you do?" Brooke asked after they had ordered their dinners.

Part of him wanted to tell her the truth, but she was an educated woman, and the truth wasn't good enough. "I'm starting a new job tomorrow in a salon on Fifth Avenue... as a beauty consultant."

"Really? Which salon?" she asked.

"Hollywood Hair," Jeremy said.

"I've heard of them," Brooke said. "Isn't that the salon where all you have to do is tell the hairstylist what movie star you want to look like?"

"That's the one."

"Do you know those men?" Brooke asked, nodding her head toward a table at the other end of the room. "They keep looking at us."

Jeremy turned halfway in his chair and glanced quickly behind him, trying to appear nonchalant. But he saw Detective Jackson, and the two of them locked eyes for a moment. The detective smirked and held his glass up. Sitting across from Detective Jackson, blowing on his soup, was his partner. He had his spoon in one hand and a pencil in the other.

Jeremy started to answer Brooke, but was interrupted by the arrival of their dinners. He felt no sense of urgency at the presence of the detectives. He was doing nothing wrong.

Two waiters balanced the round serving tray. The meals were quite tall, and Jeremy was impressed by their skill in serving the dishes without allowing them to tip over. Jeremy's hamburger was ordinary in every way—nothing towering about it. But his Eiffel Tower of french fries defied gravity and nature. The french fries were intertwined in an intricate waffle pattern and reached a height of eleven inches above the table, resembling with remarkable accuracy the famous Paris landmark. Though Brooke's dinner was a less faithful historic recreation—it looked nothing like Pisa's tilted tourist trap—it was taller. The Leaning Tower of Pizza stood a proud foot and a half, eighteen inches of melted cheese, tomato sauce, pepperoni, and mushrooms on a rigid dough frame. It was steaming hot, and sauce dripping from the top gave it the appearance of a volcano about to blow.

"Wow!" Jeremy said.

"Wow!" Brooke agreed.

Brooke and Jeremy could no longer see each other. He tried to look around his french fries but her face was blocked by her pizza. They were both lost in solitude behind their sculpted culinary masterpieces, and had no alternative but to eat their way to freedom and each other. Consuming these vertical victuals was no easy feat, and required expertise with the cutlery provided as well as complete concentration. A wrong move could topple the meal and ruin a shirt or blouse. Neither of them spoke for almost ten minutes. When they could finally see over their meals it was like the lifting of a great weight. Brooke smiled at Jeremy from across her dinner's melting horizon.

"What were we talking about?" she asked.

"I don't remember," Jeremy said.

"Oh," she said, "I was asking about those men." She pointed to the table, now empty.

Her very being exuded honesty, her smile was mesmerizing, and Jeremy knew that he could confide in her. He told her about the man with the bushy black mustache and the mysterious envelope, about Claude and the Empire State Building and losing his job, about his trip to the hospital and the Korean grocer and his job interview and the boy who might have had a gun and his letter to the Vice President of Promotions, and about Mr. Valkof and Detective Jackson and his new job at Hollywood Hair, where he not only wasn't a beauty consultant but would tomorrow begin sweeping hair and wiping down tanning booths for cash, six dollars an hour. Jeremy waited for Brooke to laugh in disbelief at his story, but she didn't.

She stood up, walked to his side of the table, and with

unbearable slowness leaned over and kissed him tenderly on the cheek. Her breath warmed his face. She smelled exactly as he imagined she would. He couldn't place it, didn't know if it was her perfume or shampoo or something else, but the air around her made Jeremy think of honey. Brooke went back to her chair and sat.

The waiter came by with dessert menus, but Brooke didn't need to see one. They would share the strawberry shortcake.

"I knew it," Brooke said.

"What?" Jeremy asked, fighting down the blush her kiss had elicited.

"That you were the one. Not right away, but after you kept coming and ordering those beautiful strawberries, I knew I'd found someone who shared a piece of my soul."

"You knew that from my ordering strawberries?"

"Those aren't just strawberries," Brooke said. "Some people order yogurt, or malteds, but not you. Every day you went for the real thing. The raw honesty of those tremendous strawberries. Sometimes after work I wondered what kind of person would order them day after day. And now I know. Do you have any idea how rare your kind of honesty is? You are pure, Jeremy Keller. I can tell when someone has an honest heart, and you do. People may not think you can tell a lot about a person by the strawberries he eats, but they're wrong."

"I don't know if I would go that far," Jeremy said.

"You don't? Then how come you just opened up to me like this? Telling me about your problems, your secrets? I had no way to check on you. I wasn't going to walk into Hollywood Hair to confirm your story. You didn't have to tell me the truth, but you did. Laugh if you want, but the strawberries don't lie."

The waiter returned with a tall, thin strawberry shortcake and two spoons on a silver plate.

"I heard they have the best shortcake," Brooke said. "That's why I picked this place. I knew you'd love it."

The cake did look good. Jeremy searched his memory, trying without success to conjure in his mind the taste of the fruit that he hadn't touched since he was a boy.

Brooke put her hand on top of his. Her skin was soft and warm. With her other hand she carved a spoonful of cake and chunks of strawberry. She reached across the table to feed Jeremy.

Jeremy closed his lips around the cake on the spoon. The chunks of strawberry had a rich tang, and he immediately recalled the flavor from his childhood. She fed him a second spoonful, looking into his eyes as she did. As Jeremy lost consciousness and fell from his chair he knew that nothing had ever tasted so sweet.

Chapter 13

Jeremy was dreaming.

He was in a tunnel he didn't recognize. The tunnel's walls were organically ridged, like a ribcage. In a rhythm consistent with breathing the walls expanded—allowing him to stand at full height—and contracted—forcing him to duck his head. There were eyes up ahead in the darkness, a wall of white with black dots staring back at him. Looking down at his own hand Jeremy realized that he was holding a gun, and he pointed it at the mass of eyes. He walked closer. The eyes had bodies now. First he saw the giant frogs—the tunnel was not as dark as before, or his vision had adjusted from his being submerged for so long. The frogs didn't attack. They spread out around him. He couldn't count them. Viewed from close up like this they weren't as menacing. Jeremy lowered the gun to his side. As soon as his guard dropped the frogs hopped at him. He tried to fight them off but they knocked the gun from his hand—it landed in water. Their tongues shot out and wrapped him up. He couldn't move his arms, but his hands were still free. There was a shotgun next to him on the wet ground, and Jeremy grabbed it. In an instant the frogs were gone. The shotgun had frightened them away. Then the rats appeared. They were so big he didn't need to bend down to look them directly in their red eyes. One ran at him. It jumped, moving through the air in slow motion. Jeremy pulled the shotgun's trigger but nothing happened. He tried again but it was no use—the weapon wasn't loaded. The slowly soaring rat became two rats, then four, multiplying so that by the time they landed on him there were dozens of the enormous rodents. They were biting his middle, eating him. On the tunnel's ceiling crawled roaches as big as humans. He heard the underground people getting closer, their deformed laughter growing louder as the rats continued to eat him up.

Jeremy awoke slowly and cried out from the ache in his stomach. Nothing was more intense than new pain. Drunks developed a tolerance for alcohol, needing to consume progressively more to approach the pleasure of that first buzz. Drugs too could let a person down—crack addicts smoked as much of the stuff they could find in the futile effort to return to the feeling of that first high. To some even sex grew stale, sending lovers in search of satisfaction to strangers or bizarre extremes to capture the pure ecstasy of that first time. But pain always delivered. Every head cold drowned out the memory of the one previous, each new migraine was the worst ever. Someone who had broken bones and ripped ligaments and had surgery and experienced the harshest suffering generally available to humankind still screamed and hopped around upon stubbing a toe as if it were the greatest possible injury.

Jeremy felt the onset of a stomach cramp, but took careful, long breaths, and fought it off. It wasn't nausea. It was an emptiness, an odd hunger, unaccompanied by any appetite for food. His eyes were still closed, his lashes wet and stuck together. When his eyes finally opened they did so reluctantly. The sunlight was intense through the white nylon shade. A needle was in his left arm, taped just above his wrist and connected by a clear tube to a bag hanging next to his bed. Chrome railings raised on both sides of the bed and to his right a beige curtain preventing him from seeing the room's exit made Jeremy feel trapped.

A man in a white coat walked into the hospital room, pulled the curtain back so Jeremy's bed was no longer hidden, and went to the window and opened the shade. He had curly blond hair and a slight limp. "How are you feeling?" he asked Jeremy. The light from the sun was so strong the circular fluorescent bulb on the ceiling added nothing.

"What happened to me?" Jeremy asked.

The man paced, dragging his leg a bit, and scratched his head. "First we didn't know what it was. You gave us a nice scare—a few of our doctors were sure it was an exotic illness imported here through some African delicacy at the restaurant, or maybe one of those flesh-eating bacterias. We'd never seen anything quite like it. Then we thought it was food poisoning, but finally we realized that it was a severe allergic reaction. We had to pump your stomach."

"I don't remember anything after eating the cake."

"Well," the man said, "it's all people around here are talking about. You ruined dinner for more than fifty people. The restaurant had to be shut down, you know, for testing. And the Board of Health had to investigate. You even made this morning's paper, but not the front page. Not that page five of the *Daily News* is anything to sneeze at. Do you want to read the article?"

"No," Jeremy said.

"Really, it's no problem. I'll just go get the paper."

"No, thank you, but I don't want to see it."

"It's nothing to be embarrassed about," the man said. "Everyone gets fifteen minutes of fame. You just happened to be unconscious for yours."

"Am I going to be all right?" Jeremy asked. He was feeling stronger.

The man removed the intravenous tube from Jeremy's arm. "You're fine," he said.

"Are you a doctor?"

"No," the man said, placing a band-aid over the bruised area on Jeremy's forearm. "I'm a nurse."

"A nurse?"

"A man can be a nurse."

"Oh," Jeremy said.

"It's a noble profession, taking care of people. There's nothing wrong with being a male nurse."

"I didn't say there was," Jeremy said.

"Good."

"Where are my clothes?" Jeremy was wearing a thin hospital dress. The pain in his stomach had mostly subsided.

"They had to be burned."

"You burned my clothes?"

"Yes."

"You burned my clothes?"

"We had to," the man who was a nurse and proud of it said. "We didn't know if you had one of those viruses, you know, the ones brought over by lab monkeys that infect a whole Midwestern town. Those viruses are a nasty business. If they spread to the general population, well, in a city like New York millions of people could die. And we'd probably have to nuke Manhattan just to save the rest of the country. So we burned your clothes. We kept you isolated until we determined it was just something you ate."

"But by then you'd already burned my clothes," Jeremy said, catching on.

"Yes. It was unfortunate, but a small price to pay for safety and the continuance of the human race," the nurse said.

"What happened to my date? The woman I was with?"

The nurse didn't know.

Jeremy's wallet and watch and keys were in the top drawer of the nightstand next to his bed. The hospital staff had been kind enough not to incinerate them along with his clothes. It was almost eleven. Jeremy was late for work. He was supposed to start a new job at ten today at Hollywood Hair. And he had an appointment at high noon—that is, a quarter after one—with the man with the bushy mustache. He asked the nurse when he would be able to leave, what medicine, if any, he needed to take, and when he could see a doctor.

The nurse told him that he didn't need to see a doctor. They were all away since it was Friday and almost two feet of snow had recently accumulated upstate and in Vermont—it was perfect weather for skiing, and it wasn't like Jeremy was dying or anything. And he wouldn't have to come back and see them on Monday because, as it turned out, his insurance was expiring today—the grace period from his former company's carrier had ended. He really should have been out of the room hours earlier, but the nurse would fudge the records for him—that was the kind of guy he was. Jeremy wouldn't have to pay for the extra time. The doctors were sure he would be all right, the nurse said. He should avoid spicy foods for a few days and try to get some rest. They only left the nurse with one specific instruction for Jeremy: no more strawberries.

"How do I get home?" Jeremy asked.

"How do you mean?" the nurse asked.

"You burned all my clothes. I can't go running outside wearing this."

The nurse saw in his wisdom that this was a real problem, but the hospital wasn't in the practice of providing wardrobes for people just because they had been mistaken for carriers of some aggressive plague. Still, the nurse was an exceptionally generous soul, and would see if he couldn't find something for Jeremy to wear. He left the room and returned just a few seconds later. Bundled in his arms was a janitor's slate gray jumpsuit and black rubber boots.

"Here you go," the nurse said.

"You want me to wear that?"

"It's all I could find," the nurse said. He held the jumpsuit out. Stitched in cursive on the pocket of the suit's breast was the janitor's name: *Buddy*. "Buddy isn't in until the evening shift. By then you'll be gone, and I'll be off, and no one will be the wiser."

"You want me to steal the janitor's uniform?"

"Steal is an awful word," the nurse said. "I prefer 'borrow.'"

"Do you want me to bring it back when I'm done borrowing it?" Jeremy asked.

"Heavens no," the nurse said. "I could get fired. Stealing from the hospital isn't looked upon kindly. Not to mention Buddy's violent temper."

"Buddy's violent temper?"

"Yes," the nurse said. "He was suspended once for slashing an intern's tires with a screwdriver. But, if you ask me, the intern had it coming."

"Maybe this isn't such a good idea," Jeremy said.

"Don't be silly," the nurse said.

"No, I'll call my brother and ask him to bring me some clothes." Jeremy was lucky. Not everyone had a family to fall back on.

"Here," the nurse said, holding out the jumpsuit with discoloration on the arms. "Take it. Everything will be fine."

Jeremy wouldn't take the jumpsuit or the shoes. He knew that nothing good could come from this. "You want me to walk out of this hospital with a jumpsuit belonging to a temperamental janitor named Buddy, and you think everything will be fine? His name is stitched right there for everyone to see. This isn't a sitcom, you know. This is my life. I'm not going to get caught up in wacky misadventures, posing as a janitor and hiding from a screwdriver-wielding maniac just to please you—this isn't *Three's Company*. I'll call my brother."

The nurse looked down at the floor. "I was only trying to help."

It was true. The nurse had been willing to risk his own job to aid Jeremy. He was a compassionate man. If more people were like this nurse, if kindness weren't bordering on extinction, what a wonderful world it would be.

"Thank you for your help," Jeremy said, "but I'll wait for my brother."

"I never wanted to be a nurse, anyway," the nurse said. "Even my mother made fun of me. 'What kind of man becomes a nurse?'"

"There's nothing wrong with a man being a nurse," Jeremy said.

"There isn't?"

"Of course not," Jeremy said. "What could be more noble than helping people?"

"You're right," the nurse said, a smile returning to his

young face. And with that he scooped up the janitor's uniform and boots and left the room.

Jeremy called Marc. It wasn't easy for Jeremy to get through to his brother. Marc didn't like to be disturbed at work, and the mention of Jeremy's name not only didn't inspire confidence in Marc's secretary, but recognition either. She hadn't heard of Marc having any brother, and didn't want to upset her boss by interrupting his meeting for some salesman using this trick to get past her. She was the crucial first line of defense. If Jeremy were selling something he should tell her. She would make sure Mr. Keller got the message. Jeremy assured her that he was indeed Marc's brother and as proof described a birthmark on Marc's hip. It was shaped like a quarter moon. Marc's receptionist knew of no such birthmark, but then she wasn't privy to all of his secrets. Wasn't that proof enough? He must be Marc's brother if he knew about a birthmark of which even Marc's trusted assistant had no knowledge. She was skeptical. Anyone could invent a birthmark—it didn't prove anything.

Jeremy, his voice writhing in agony, told her that he had a contagious flesh-eating virus and would not live much longer without a skin transplant. His brother was the only suitable donor. She didn't believe him. Did he think she was an idiot or something? She sympathized with his plight, but took her responsibilities seriously. Jeremy commended her for her discipline and loyalty. His brother was fortunate to have such a steadfast colleague. She was right to have doubts. But if she checked the paper she would see he was sincere. If he were telling the truth, if the man with the mysterious illness on page five of the *Daily News* had the same last name as her boss, wouldn't it be in both their best interests for her to put him through to Marc? Jeremy was on hold for several minutes. A recording tried to sell him opera tickets. Marc's receptionist was both apologetic and sympathetic when she returned to the phone. How could she have known he was telling the truth? It wasn't the first time someone had called claiming near-death in order to talk to Mr. Keller. It had all the makings of a ruse. She was only doing her job. Jeremy understood, and would not hold it against her.

Jeremy had to tell his brother the story over the phone. Not the whole story, but the part about losing his job at Dubasky and Cohen and eating strawberry shortcake and being late for the first day of his new job at Hollywood Hair, and having no clothes on account of the epidemic popularity of books and movies depicting outbreaks of catastrophic diseases. He didn't tell Marc unnecessary details, didn't mention the man with the bushy mustache or their upcoming meeting. Marc arrived just over an hour later with a paper shopping bag, and gave Jeremy sneakers, jeans, a sweatshirt, and an old red winter coat. Marc was wearing a tailored navy blue suit. He looked like a stocky and more masculine version of a department store mannequin.

"I was in a very important negotiation," Marc said. "I hope you appreciate this."

"Thanks for coming," Jeremy said.

"Take this, for cab fare home," Marc said, slipping Jeremy a crisp twenty-dollar bill.

"Thank you."

"What is it with you?" Marc asked.

"There's nothing with me," Jeremy said.

"Oh, there's something," Marc said. "There's always something. Nobody gets fired for nothing."

Jeremy dressed as they spoke. "I didn't deserve to get

fired. There was a misunderstanding. These things happen."

"These things don't just happen," Marc said. "They happen to *you*."

"I don't want to argue," Jeremy said. "I'm already late for work."

"Jeremy, you're thirty years old. What kind of a life is sweeping hair?"

"It's honest work, and it's temporary."

"That's what you said when you dropped out of school and started working in a mailroom. 'It's temporary.' When are you going to do something with your life?"

"I have a feeling something big is going to happen soon," Jeremy said.

"You've been saying that for years," Marc said.

"But this time I'm right. I know it."

"Life is going to pass you by while you wait for something big to happen," Marc said. "I've made a phone call..."

"Who'd you call?" Jeremy didn't like his brother meddling in his affairs.

"You know I usually don't do this sort of thing," Marc said, handing Jeremy a business card, "but I know the president of this company, and he owes me one. He's agreed to hire you."

"I have a job—"

"—Sweeping hair. Jeremy, you're brighter than that. You have to be. I don't want to hear any more on the subject. You start Monday morning. Be early and wear a tie."

"But—"

"—And remember," Marc said, "I'm doing you a favor. And I never do favors. This is a real opportunity. So, for once in your life, try not to screw it up."

Chapter 14

Jeremy didn't see why he couldn't have it all. Although he was possessed by no ardent desire to be a captain of industry, had no secret designs on becoming a corporate Napoleon, he was not without material needs. Destiny had given no indication in all these weeks that it would pay the rent, and as Jeremy achieved whatever greatness waited out there like some beast in the jungle he would need to somehow earn a living. Why not earn a good one? A career with responsibilities and potential for growth was better than pushing a broom and wiping sweat from the plastic benches of tanning booths. Besides, he didn't have the energy to explain to the woman who had hired him at Hollywood Hair why he hadn't made it in on time for his first day. It would be easier to never see her again. And there was something persuasive about Marc's offer, an authority in his voice, a twinkle in his eye as he spoke that Jeremy could not resist. Accepting his help wasn't difficult. For all Jeremy knew, this opportunity delivered by his brother was as much an act of fate as was his encounter with the man with the bushy mustache—the logic of the universe was dark and mysterious.

The clothes Marc had provided were too tight and wafted in a five-foot radius around its wearer the scent of mothballs. The jeans and sweatshirt and sneakers and coat were not Marc's. He was bigger than Jeremy, and nothing he owned smelled like anything. This month Chipping In had organized a clothing drive to help the homeless, but Jeremy knew his brother wouldn't have brought him a stranger's antiquated apparel. There had to be some other explanation. The dirt on the red winter coat had a soaked-in permanence—it was beyond washing. Touching it didn't soil one's hands; it was so filthy it was clean again. Jeremy was a few blocks from Washington Square Park, and walked with caution to prevent his jeans from riding up.

Flags in NYU purple hung limply from the sides of buildings. It was a cold and clear day, and negotiating the crowded sidewalk was not for the inexperienced or indecisive. Hardened New Yorkers knew how important it was to keep moving, to be alert and sensitive to the flow of human traffic. Sudden stops and starts and changes of direction were required to get anywhere. It was necessary to skip and leap and lunge to not collide with the other hurried people who were themselves caught up in the intricate dance of lunging and leaping and skipping. Jeremy was reminded of his high school days, of the cramped hallways and the impossible rush to get from one class to the next in the five minutes allotted. His classes had been in opposite ends of the tremendous building, its rooms numbered non-sequentially and with no particular guiding principle, making it impossible to find a room in the four stories shaped like a figure eight by any process other than trial and error. Jeremy had often felt lost, and didn't remember ever being early for a single class in all his time at the high school.

It was nice to know that those days were behind him. His years at Dubasky and Cohen were also a mere memory. Jeremy wasn't the same person, locked into a mailroom for all eternity. He was not only meeting the man with the bushy mustache in less than an hour, but had a new career waiting for him on Monday morning. He saw himself in an office, asking his secretary with proper paternal politeness for a cup of coffee, two sugars, one cream—he didn't drink coffee, but resolved to start, if only for the sake of appearances and the furtherance of his career, which already in his mind took on a significance of monolithic proportions. All the pieces were coming together as one.

An elderly couple walked in front of Jeremy. They must have had between them two hundred years. They and their growing numbers were a new kind of old, a modern phenomenon. Secluded, long-bearded Russians eating yogurt and living forever were not the exception any longer but now increasingly the rule; celebrating a hundredth birthday was barely news—everyone was doing it. The woman leaned on a wired shopping cart, more scraping across the concrete than rolling. Her husband had a hand on the cart, as if he were reluctant to allow his wife to steer without his direction. They wore long coats and scarves and stopped at every window, taking extra time to look at the display for the store that sold nothing but sneakers, which though marketed to teenagers were affordable to none with less than a six-figure salary or a corporate expense account. Jeremy wasn't yet late, but was too excited about his destined meeting and his new job to have patience with the molasses mobility of the pruned pair. He tried to squeeze past them.

The oncoming throng did not make room for him, and Jeremy scooted back behind the dawdling couple to avoid being trampled. They didn't pick up the pace, and he had to wait almost five minutes until they reached the end of the block before he could get around them. He crossed at the corner, walked past a cigar bar that, though not yet one in the afternoon, was filled to capacity with men and women puffing and gesturing dramatically with oversized stogies. A beautiful woman with black hair to her shoulders sat on a stool at a tall round table drinking Evian spring water. Her features were so very delicate, her nose so precise and symmetrical, she seemed to Jeremy to be an artificial exaggeration of feminine beauty. Her bionic nose and pasty white skin belonged in a gallery or a science museum—their absolute perfection couldn't have had organic origins. Even toking on the titanic cigar she held between her fingers she was angelic, sweet and innocent.

Jeremy walked halfway up the block and had come within sight of the still distant trees of Washington Square Park when he saw the car. It wasn't just a car—it was a Mercedes Benz. And not just a Mercedes, but the kind Janis Joplin sang about with such boundless enthusiasm on television commercials. Janis was right. A car like this could make amends for most anything. It was a stunning red, a red unlike any before seen—there was probably a patent on the color. Jeremy did not normally notice things like expensive cars, or pay them much attention, but his pending occupational advances made all things possible. He wouldn't have to write such works of art off as out of his reach again. What a car! He leaned close to the driver's side window adjacent to the sidewalk and cupped his hand next to his eyes to block out the sun's glare. The instrument controls by the steering wheel and on the contoured dashboard were like something out of a science fiction movie.

Just then there came from deep within the car, from somewhere under the gleaming hood, a synthesized, booming voice. "You are standing too close to the car," it said.

Jeremy was startled by the voice, by its smooth and easy manner. But he wasn't touching the car, and continued to look through the window.

Five seconds passed before the car alarm again addressed him. "You are standing too close to the car. Please step away from the car."

Jeremy was truly impressed by the alarm's sensitivity and well-spoken warning. He peered through the back door window. It was roomy, perfect for a family or for taking long trips.

The car sounded a loud burst of beeps and honks and sirens for a ten-second duration. "This car is being stolen," it said. "Call the police."

Though the voice and siren could be heard up and down the block, people on both sides of the narrow street walked past without breaking stride, ignoring the car like so much city background noise. If it were being stolen it was no business of theirs—its owner was certain to have insurance. These alarms were often set off by passing trucks and vibrations from thunderstorms and mild breezes, and the hectic pace of city life didn't permit hearing them as anything but incessant nuisances.

The car alarm again told Jeremy to step away from the car. He laughed. Even at his lowest he wouldn't have taken orders from an inanimate object, and now that his destiny and a career both beckoned him he had no intention of bowing to the car's demands. When he bought his own luxury automobile he would have to remember not to purchase such a pointless alarm.

"Get away from the car," a soft, feminine voice behind him said.

Jeremy thought for the briefest moment that it was the car alarm speaking, throwing its voice and imitating with uncanny accuracy the inflection of a young woman, a mechanical and marvelous ventriloquist.

"I said back away from my car," the woman said.

Jeremy turned away from the car. It was the beautiful woman from the cigar bar, the one with the sculpted angel's face. She wore a teal suit that clung to her generous curves and revealed legs no less perfect than her nose. She was a sight, a wonder of aesthetic achievement on a par with her red Mercedes. Both deserved admiration as feats of hard work and advanced engineering. The woman suppressed a shiver. She must have rushed out of the cigar bar, because she wasn't wearing a coat, despite temperatures approaching the freezing mark.

"What do you think you're doing?" she asked, brandishing a small squeeze bottle of Bausch & Lomb contact lens saline solution at Jeremy.

"I'm just looking," he said.

"Don't look from so close," she said.

"I'm thinking of buying one of these," Jeremy said.

"Get away from my car," the woman said.

The car alarm echoed her sentiment. "Please step away from the car," it said

Jeremy complied with the car's wishes, and stepped away.

"Don't come any closer to me," the woman said, aiming the green and white bottle of saline solution at Jeremy.

"I can't step away from the car unless you give me somewhere to go."

"I'm not kidding," she said. "I'll use this."

"You're going to squirt me with saline solution for contact lenses?"

"This isn't saline solution." She waved it like a gun.

"It says on the bottle that it's saline solution," Jeremy said.

"I know what it says on the bottle," she said. "But it isn't saline solution."

"I didn't do anything to your car. I was just looking. There's no need to salinate me."

"I told you this isn't saline solution," the woman said, the edge on her voice daring him to defy her. "It's acid."

"You have acid in your bottle of saline solution?"

"Yes," she said.

While they spoke people continued to walk past, no one noticing or bothering to stop.

"You don't have acid in that bottle." Jeremy had been bullied by the young boy on the subway platform claiming to have a gun, but would not fall for such a bluff again.

"It is acid," she said, "and you're going to stay here until the police come."

"You're crazy," Jeremy said. "First of all, I didn't do anything wrong, and second, you don't have anything in that bottle but salty water."

"I do too—" she said, but was interrupted by the ringing of a phone from inside the short jacket of her teal suit. "Wait a second," she said to him, then pulled out a phone no bigger than the palm of her hand. She flipped open the bottom of the phone and spoke into it.

"Hello?" she inquired. "Peter, how are you? ...I'm

doing well. And the kids? ...Tonight? ...That would be great..."

Jeremy could see that she was busy, and began to walk away.

"Hold on, Peter," the woman said into the phone, then to Jeremy, "Where do you think you're going?"

"I don't want to disturb your call," he said. "I'll just be on my way now."

"Oh no you won't," she said, and shook the bottle of saline solution.

Jeremy ignored her. He couldn't acknowledge the rambling of a deluded woman. No matter how sophisticated she looked, she was just another crazy person pretending to have some weapon against the horrors of the world. He had gained only five feet in distance from her when a stream of yellow-white liquid splattered the sidewalk in front of him. It bubbled and fizzled. The woman was standing a few feet from him, pointing the Bausch & Lomb bottle at his face. "I have to go, Peter," she said into the phone. "I'll call you later." She made a kissing sound into the receiver and then folded the phone and put it back into her suit jacket's interior pocket, fixing her covert weapon on Jeremy as she did.

"You'll go when I say you can go," she said to Jeremy.

Jeremy watched the streak of acid on the ground out of the corner of his eye. It continued to crackle, and smoke came off of it and was carried past him by the gentle wind. It smelled like rotten eggs.

"I told you it wasn't saline solution," the woman said, reveling in the success of her surprise tactic and the fear on Jeremy's face.

If Jeremy tried to run she might spray him. He wasn't

fast enough to get away. "You did tell me. I should have listened."

"This bottle contains a powerful concentration of hydrochloric acid," she told him, with obvious pride. "It'll melt your eyes in seconds. It'll eat right through that disgusting coat of yours, right down to the skin."

"I don't want any trouble," Jeremy said.

"You should have thought of that before you messed with my car."

"I was just looking. I'm sorry."

"What is it with you people?" she asked.

Jeremy hadn't realized he belonged to any group so easily categorized. "I'm sorry. What people?"

"I pay my taxes," she said. The bottle of acid was still leveled at his face.

"That's very good of you," Jeremy said, without sarcasm.

"I pay my taxes," she said again. "And I give to charity when they call on the phone. It's not my fault you're dressed like that."

"I don't blame you," Jeremy said.

"I'm supporting one of those children. I forget which country she lives in, but you know the one. Sally Struthers is always talking about those poor villages on TV."

"That's very kind of you." Jeremy's whole body shook.

"'Feed the children,' they tell me, and I do. I'm not against welfare. I know you people need to eat. But I work hard." She stepped closer, the bottle of hydrochloric just inches from Jeremy's face, and screamed, "Can't you just leave me alone?"

Jeremy shrank back, shielded his eyes with his hand, and crouched to make himself a smaller target, his other hand holding the base of a parking meter. The woman towered over him. "Please don't hurt me," Jeremy said, his voice breaking up. He was sure this was it. He would go down like this, sniveling for mercy, with destiny right around the corner.

She was silent for a moment, then continued, no longer screaming, "I can't go anywhere without someone begging me for money. I just want to be left alone."

"I was wrong to be so close to your car," Jeremy said.

"That's right," the woman said. She abandoned her threatening posture and gave him more room.

"I didn't do any damage. I'm sorry, really, I am."

"You shouldn't have done it," she said.

"I know," Jeremy said, standing up.

"You could've gotten hurt. You shouldn't do this kind of thing in New York. It's a dangerous place."

"I know," Jeremy said. "Can I go now?"

"There are crazy people everywhere," she said. "People think you're stealing their car and you're liable to get shot. Not everyone is going to be as rational as I am."

"I got lucky," Jeremy agreed.

"You need to watch yourself."

"I'll be careful," Jeremy said, backing away.

"Take care of yourself," she said, with real concern.

"You too," he said, before turning and walking with great speed down the block. Jeremy could hear her speaking into her phone as he reached the corner and saw the park.

"Yes, Peter ...Nine-thirty is perfect ...Don't you worry. I'll make the reservations."

Chapter 15

Jeremy passed the great arch at the northern entrance to Washington Square Park. Despite the growing strength of the wind and the resulting chill, people were taking full advantage of the park's facilities. Not that the park had anything extraordinary to offer. It was like many of the so-called parks in the city, covered by more paved ground than grass. In the middle of the park, off center and to the west, was a kind of poor man's theater in the round. There was no stage, just a few descending steps connected in a wide circle, where in the warmer months jugglers and unicyclists and mimes and others fancying themselves artists sought to separate audiences from their spare change. Good-natured barking could be heard from the enclosed dog run at the southwest end as animals delighted in smelling each other and the supervising humans gossiped and shook hands, the frolicking canines and their upright counterparts each growling and sniffing in the manner appropriate to their species.

The park was surrounded on all sides by New York University. Six black men dressed only slightly better than Jeremy played soccer on the asphalt, using as goal posts on one end a metal trashcan and a worn canvas backpack, at the other end an empty forty-ounce bottle of beer and a stack of old books. Their breath in the cold air was visible evidence of their exertion. A young white man in an olive business suit and black overcoat was pretending to sleep on a bench while a younger white woman with an expensive camera took pictures. He posed and she snapped, both of them laughing. The young Chinese couple on the next bench over held each other tight and kissed with a passion that in most public places demanded at least a second look.

Washington Square was a sort of haven for anyone who didn't fit into the neat structure of society. Pierced noses and eyebrows and body parts both more tender and less revealed were as common here as were canasta and mah-jongg and cream cheese and lox on certain stretches of Miami Beach. Two well-dressed men walked along the sidewalk across from the library, gazing deeply into each other's eyes, hands clasped. A black man with a disheveled thick head of hair and a scratchy beard, wearing an ancient green army jacket, approached Jeremy, who was himself across from the library and on his way to the southeast corner. It was five minutes past one, and there was as of yet no man with the bushy mustache.

"Psst," the man in the army coat said. He glanced quickly to both sides.

Jeremy ignored him and continued to walk.

The man ran ahead of Jeremy and turned around, forcing Jeremy to pass him. "Psst," he said.

Jeremy said nothing.

"Smoke?" the man asked, in a loud whisper.

"I don't smoke," Jeremy said.

The man walked backwards, keeping up with Jeremy, and asked again, "Smoke?"

"I don't have any cigarettes," Jeremy said.

"No," the man said. "Do you want a smoke?"

"No, thank you," Jeremy said.

"Not cigarettes," the man said. "I got the good stuff."

"Enjoy it," Jeremy said, immediately regretting the anger in his voice—it hadn't been an easy day, not with his brief hospital stay and his encounter with the red Mercedes. "You have the good stuff?" he asked, trying to make it up to the man who for all Jeremy knew had risked his life for his country and the cause of freedom.

"You bet I do."

Jeremy still didn't see the man with the bushy mustache, and stopped walking. "If you don't mind my asking, what exactly is the good stuff?"

In a confiding tone the bearded veteran said, "You know, the good stuff."

"Oh, the good stuff." Jeremy tried to sound agreeable, but still didn't know what precisely they were talking about.

"You want some?" the man asked.

"No, thank you."

The retired war hero had a look of supreme dejection on his face.

"It isn't that I wouldn't like some good stuff," Jeremy said, trying to raise his spirits. "And it's nothing personal."

"Sure it isn't," the man said, not believing a word.

"Really," Jeremy said. "If this was a month ago, back when I was smoking the good stuff all the time, you'd be the first one I'd come to." Little lies were the fabric of civilization. Brutal honesty was an apt term, and a fib in the service of easing tensions and feelings was to Jeremy always justified.

"You want some?" the man asked, encouraged.

"Well, the truth is, I've been trying to cut down."

"I can let you have it for a discount."

"That's a generous offer, and a tempting one. But I have an important meeting in a few minutes. You know how it is."

"No, I don't."

"Neither do I," Jeremy admitted. "But I think I should avoid the good stuff until after. I'm a little nervous."

"You'll do fine," the veteran said. "Just stand up straight."

"Thank you," Jeremy said, thrusting his chest forward in an effort to appear more substantial.

The bearded man shook Jeremy's hand. "You have a good meeting."

"Good luck making a sale," Jeremy said. Sometimes he met the nicest people in the city.

Jeremy reached the corner of the park and bought a hot pretzel from a vendor. The excess salt fell away with a brush of Jeremy's hand, and he savored the first, dry bite— though his stomach no longer hurt, it was empty, and this was the only food he'd tasted since the previous evening's dinner and strawberry shortcake. He imagined that they had pumped his stomach with a black hose, the ridged, flexible kind attached to wet-dry vacuum cleaners. As he chewed he could hear his insides settling, making a satisfied shifting sound with each bite.

A squirrel scampered from a tree to the path. It blocked Jeremy's way and stared up at the pretzel, then looked him in the eye before returning its attention to his handful of hardened, twisted dough. The squirrel seemed to be trying to determine its best course of action. It leaned back on its hind legs, looking not unlike a dog begging for table scraps.

Jeremy wondered if the squirrel was capable of thought. Did it resent him his ability to buy a pretzel without having to beg for it? The squirrel was certain to have a store of nuts in a nearby tree. They were famous for their forethought—squirreling away wasn't an empty phrase. But Jeremy felt guilty watching the squirrel with its hopeful posture and beady eyes. He tossed it a small piece of pretzel. The squirrel snatched it and dashed off, without even a gesture of gratitude.

Jeremy's feet ached, and after due consideration he decided that the benches on his left would allow him the best angle of sight—he didn't want to be surprised by the man with the bushy mustache. His toes were crushed up front in the narrow sneakers provided earlier that day by his brother. Jeremy wasn't an expert on torture, but thought that making a man wear shoes too small for his feet had to rank right up there with the thumbscrew and the rack.

A few minutes passed. Jeremy checked his watch again and again, occupying himself and trying to calm his nerves by guessing where the second hand would be each time. Telling time was a skill Jeremy acquired late in life. As a child he'd owned only digital watches with plastic straps and as an adolescent his wristwatch doubled as a calculator—to this day he struggled when checking the math on a restaurant bill. He had learned the second hand and minute hand in grade school, and knew of course how to read a traditional clock, but still read them as one reads a vaguely familiar foreign language. He didn't trust his eyes when telling time, and was not usually confident in his interpretation until after his third glance. Because of this he only wore non-digital wristwatches. Part of him was determined to overcome his deficiency in this area, but mainly he was pleased and captivated on some profound level by the never-ending sweep of the second hand, its glorious arc forever counting away the minutes of the day.

"Jeremy."

Jeremy looked up from his watch, but saw no one.

"Jeremy," a voice called.

Jeremy looked around. There was nobody behind the bench, no one to his left or right, and nothing in front of him except for a few leafless tall trees on the other side of the path, in a triangle of grass and surrounded by a low wrought-iron fence.

"Jeremy," came from the trees. It was like something out of *The Wizard of Oz*. But Jeremy didn't mind if the trees spoke as long as they didn't throw apples at him.

The man with the bushy mustache leaned from behind a tree trunk. He wore a gray trench coat over his dark suit. On his head was a small black beret.

"Jeremy," he said.

"Right here," Jeremy said.

The man with the bushy mustache walked very quickly and with a short hop was over the fence. He sat next to Jeremy on the park bench.

"You smell like mothballs," he said.

"I know."

"I knew you lost your job," the man said, "but I had no idea things were this bad."

"They're not," Jeremy said. "It's a long story. What were you doing behind that tree?"

"I've been watching you."

"I know. That's how all of this started."

"No, I mean I've been watching you these last few minutes. To make sure you weren't followed."

"Who would want to follow me?" Jeremy asked. "I mean, besides you."

"You'd be surprised," the man with the bushy mustache said. "You can't be too careful."

"I suppose not."

"I guess you're wondering why I was following you."

"The question had occurred to me."

"Well, I can't tell you. Not here."

"Why not?"

"They might be listening. I had no way to check for a bug, no time to examine the surrounding benches."

"Who might be listening?" Jeremy asked.

"I can't say, in case they're listening. I wouldn't want them to know I'm on to them."

"I see." Things were more complex than Jeremy had imagined.

"We are standing at the edge of history, you and I," the man with the bushy mustache said.

"We are?"

"We most certainly are."

"What's your name?"

"Why do you want to know that?"

"I just don't know what to call you. You know my name. Shouldn't I know yours?"

"The less you know the better."

"I want to know whatever there is to know."

"When the time is right. When the time is right. For now you can call me Eagle."

"Why Eagle?" Jeremy felt silly saying the name, addressing the man as one might address a winged superhero. Jeremy almost laughed as he pictured his question printed in a comic book dialogue bubble.

"I can't say."

"Why did you ask me to meet you here, if you weren't going to tell me anything?" Jeremy asked.

"I didn't ask you," the man said. "I wanted to talk to you in your apartment yesterday morning, where it was safe. But you had to insist on a public place, remember? So here we are."

"Here we are," Jeremy agreed. Destiny wasn't as forthcoming as he had hoped.

"I brought something for you." The man with the bushy mustache pulled a familiar manila envelope from inside his coat. *Jeremy Keller* was on its face in blue ink. He placed the envelope on Jeremy's lap. "Take this."

Jeremy stared down at the envelope. It had the same tape on it as when he'd first seen it months ago, the day after he first spotted the man following him. He was certain it hadn't been opened in all this time. He tugged at the tape—nothing would stop him from learning its contents now.

"Don't do that here. They might be watching."

Jeremy restrained himself. "You said yesterday there was no need for melodramatic precautions."

"This isn't melodrama. And things have changed since yesterday."

"I didn't realize," Jeremy said.

"It isn't your fault," the man said. "You'll have to get used to being cautious. Open the envelope only when you're home, away from prying eyes. In it is something you will need if you're going to join me."

"Did you steal this from my office?"

"Yes. I thought you weren't ready, that I had made a mistake in choosing you. In matters as grave as these, hasty decisions can have terrible consequences."

"But you followed me again, when I ran into the grocery store. And you're here now," Jeremy said.

"I followed you more than that. Maybe a half dozen times. I had to be sure that you were what I thought you were."

"And now you're sure?"

"There can be no doubt," the man said. "I have to be getting back. I have a meeting at two."

"What should I do?"

"I'll contact you. The conditions will be right next week. Everything will become clear."

"It will?"

"Don't worry," the man said. "Go home and open the envelope. The first stage of your initiation is inside. Wear it well, wear it always, and trust only those who wear the same."

"I don't understand."

"I have already divulged too much," the man said, getting up. "Next week." And then he turned and walked away, not looking back and disappearing from sight as quickly as he had appeared.

Jeremy was dizzy from all the new almost-information he had received. What he needed was to go home, eat some solid food, take a shower, and change into his own clothes. He held the envelope tight and walked mostly on his heels to alleviate the pain in his toes.

As Jeremy crossed the street and headed toward the subway he saw the veteran in the green army coat bent over the hood of a sky-blue sedan. The sedan was half on the curb, and the veteran's hands were cuffed behind him. A young undercover police officer with wild hair, in ripped jeans and a dirty New York Mets coat, read to the veteran from a white card: "You have the right to remain silent. Anything you say can and will be used against you in a court of law."

Chapter 16

With the shades closed and the door to his apartment bolted, Jeremy peeled the tape from his long-awaited envelope. He tried to stay calm, told himself that whatever he found inside would not come to rule him. Destiny had to be handled with care. Clumps of tissue paper and layers of bubble wrap surrounded a small gray cloth bag with drawstrings pulled tight. Removing the protective plastic took a few minutes. The man with the bushy mustache had safeguarded the bag and its contents well—Jeremy was an expert on such matters from his years of wrapping experience at Dubasky and Cohen. He ripped away more tape and unwound the bubble wrap until finally he penetrated fate's barrier and felt the softness of the bag. With trembling hands he opened it. Inside was a gold eagle, its wings spread two inches across for flight, feathers and pointy beak carved in intricate detail, a pin on the back. It was heavy, maybe solid gold.

Though Jeremy hadn't been expecting anything as obvious as a pirate's treasure map—in life X rarely marked the spot—he *was* disappointed. Even some measure of an answer would have sufficed, but examining the eagle told him nothing. All it meant to him was that he was accepted, to what he didn't know, except that its mysterious nature had to be rivaled by its importance. He was eager to learn more, but the man with the bushy mustache knew what he was doing, and Jeremy would just have to trust destiny and his new friend's judgment. Jeremy pinned the eagle on his chest, to the left, over his heart. He didn't know if this was proper, but hoped there wasn't a rule against wearing it on the wrong side. He had no wish to cause problems within the secret organization that had sought him out so enthusiastically.

He wondered how many other initiates there were. Maybe there were only a dozen people, a select few to carry on the organization's important work. Or maybe there were hundreds, even thousands of initiates around the globe, each fighting for the organization's goals in their small way. He didn't think membership was too high—Jeremy knew no one other than himself who wore such a beautiful and significant piece of jewelry. Posing with his eagle pin in front of the full-length mirror mounted on the bathroom door, Jeremy felt a new, overdue strength. The mirror was not of the highest quality, and distorted reflections to a degree, like a mirror in a fun house. Jeremy's stick-figure reflection wavered—he could never find an angle from which to view himself accurately—but his frail appearance was only an illusion. The truth, he had no doubt, was that he was part of something larger and stronger than anything he had imagined.

In a way Jeremy was happy for this last forced and secretive delay in the discovery of his life's purpose. He was approaching the final phase of his long search, that much was clear. On Monday his new professional life would begin, and at some point during the week he would meet with the man with the bushy mustache and understand what he had been chasing all this time. It seemed to Jeremy that the few days between now and then were granted to him almost by design—as a gift. He had an opportunity to begin his new life with a clean slate. There were too many dangling threads of his former existence that he wanted to tie down before getting on with the business of his destiny. With two peanut butter and jelly sandwiches in him, a more comfortable pair of sneakers, clothes that didn't smell like his grandmother's closet, and his soaring gold eagle, Jeremy was smiling as he left to go see Frank at Dubasky and Cohen.

Jeremy didn't obsess about the past—the future was too inviting. Still, in the last few months he'd had enough time to think about everything that had happened to him, to put things in their proper places, give weight in his mind to those events that most deserved it. The way his friendship with Frank had ended left him with questions he couldn't answer, and before he moved on and forever forgot the man he once was Jeremy wanted to hear from Frank's own mouth how he could have fired him, after all they'd been through together. Not that the explanation, whatever it might be, could change things. And Jeremy was fine with that—his life was bordering on his greatest expectations, and he had no regrets. To have an answer, though, to reach some closure, as they said on TV, was good for the soul, for both their souls.

It was past four on Friday, and Jeremy caught the bus that until just months earlier he had taken to work five days a week for seven years. He had never had an out-of-body experience, didn't go in for the magical claims of those who had been touched by spirits outside the range of normal human perception, but felt that it wasn't him now on the bus stuck in traffic on its way to Dubasky and Cohen. It was a vague and not altogether unpleasant sensation, an incongruity, like the first steep drop of a roller coaster, without the glee—as if part of Jeremy were left behind at the bus stop. This feeling of being left behind remained with him as he walked the three blocks to his old office building a half-hour later.

The revolving door at the building's glass front was turning at a steady rate, as Jeremy imagined it had every day since his departure. It had no reason to shut everyone out of work on his account. He hadn't expected the door or elevators or copy machines to miss him, but the people were another story. It must have been hard on them. They had lost in a moment of brutality a trusted colleague. The mailroom must have taken weeks to recover, maybe months—without Jeremy operations must have been seriously disrupted—and the company might just now be returning to a semblance of normalcy. During his empty days at home, when he wasn't watching mute talk shows or visiting Strawberry Dreams, Jeremy had occasionally fantasized of a triumphant return—if only for a visit—to Dubasky and Cohen and the mailroom. Always in these afternoon wanderings of his mind the workers cheered him, Frank hung his head and offered an embarrassed apology, which Jeremy accepted each time with the grace of one who had moved beyond the limits of their four walls.

The building had removed from its lobby the artificial tree with the hidden speakers. No songbirds welcomed Jeremy back. He never liked that tree anyway. In its place was a circular, black desk. Sitting behind the desk was a security guard, a young black man in gray with rolled up sleeves and official-looking patches, with a blue cap drawn down almost to his eyes. He was a muscular man, not taller than Jeremy but thicker in the chest and arms. The guard's chair was on a platform; he could see the entire lobby from his post, suspended like a lifeguard at a beach above those he protected. Jeremy had to pass the desk to get to the elevators.

"Excuse me, sir, I need to see your pass," the guard said, his voice high and steady.

Jeremy didn't know anything about a pass. He had never needed one before. "I'm just here to visit some friends."

"No one is allowed in the building without a pass," the guard said.

Jeremy saw that the other people entering and leaving the building had laminated pink cards clipped to their coats or hanging from their necks. "I used to work here," Jeremy said.

"I'm sorry, but without a pass I can't let you in."

"I just want to see some old friends," Jeremy said. "Can't you cut me some slack?"

"If I cut you slack I have to cut everyone slack," the guard said.

"You're not going to get in any trouble if this once someone doesn't have a pass. I'll just be a few minutes."

"Are you trying to get me fired?" the guard asked. "This may not be the best job in the world, but it's the only one I got. And the benefits are good. How do I know the company didn't send you to test me? Sure, I let you enter without a pass because I'm a nice guy, and then I'm out on the street. You gonna feed my daughter when they fire me?"

The guard was right. It was wrong of Jeremy to ask for special treatment. "How do I get a guest pass?"

"Fill out this form," the guard said, stepping down from his chair and handing over a wood clipboard with a piece of paper on it. A pen was chained to the clipboard, which was itself chained to the circular desk. It would take a thief with extraordinary ambition to make off with the valuable office supplies. The form required Jeremy to write his name, address, phone number, birthday, reason for visiting, and the names and addresses of three references—non-relatives—who could vouch for the purity of his intentions. Jeremy struggled to think of three. Mr. Valkof was one. Holly Day another. Both were easy choices since Jeremy knew their addresses as well as his own. But a third name eluded him.

"Here you go," Jeremy said, handing back the clipboard.

The guard studied the form.

"I know I only listed two references," Jeremy said, "but I'm between jobs. I hope it's not too big a problem."

"You need three," the guard said.

"I don't know anyone else, nobody who isn't related to me, nobody whose address I remember," Jeremy said.

"You must not get out much."

"Would it be so terrible if you issued me a pass anyway? Two references ought to be enough."

"Let me see what I can do," the guard said. He typed into the security station's computer. "I'm sorry, Mr. Keller, but it says here I can't admit you."

"Why not?"

"It doesn't say. I entered your name and the computer listed you as undesirable. I'm going to have to ask you to leave."

"There must be some mistake," Jeremy said. "I worked here for seven years. I just want to visit some old friends at Dubasky and Cohen."

"It isn't up to me," the guard said. "The computer says you don't get in, then you don't get in."

"Isn't there anything I can do?"

"No," the guard said.

"Then I'll just wait in the lobby for my friends to get off of work," Jeremy said.

"You need to leave the building. And I'm not allowed to let you stay out front either."

"The sidewalk is public property. I can stay there if I want to."

"The building owns that sidewalk," the guard said.

"No one can own a sidewalk."

"They own it."

"I don't care what they own."

"Don't make trouble for me," the guard said. "I don't want to get rough with you."

"What right do you have to tell me where I can and cannot go? If I want to stand out front then that's where I'll stand. Your threats don't scare me."

"I'm trying to be patient with you," the guard said. "But if you think I'm gonna risk my job, you're as crazy as you are stupid."

"Crazy or stupid, I'm not going anywhere. You just try and move me," Jeremy said. There were some principles worth fighting for.

The guard walked out from behind the desk. Hanging at his side was a nightstick and a flashlight. He removed the nightstick from his belt and slapped it into his palm. Tattooed on his flexed right forearm was a dragon breathing fire. "I don't want to hurt you. But if this is how you want it... Either way, I've got a job to do, and you're not staying."

Jeremy reconsidered. He had nothing against the guard, didn't want to tarnish the hard-working man's record with an incident that could easily be avoided. The man had a daughter, a family to support. Jeremy didn't blame him for his willingness to use violence to keep his job. It wasn't the guard's fault. Jeremy blamed the building, the city, the way events had of spiraling out of control. The guard and Jeremy were both victims. They lived in a world which, on a more or less regular basis, demanded that its inhabitants smash each other's heads with clubs. It didn't make Jeremy feel any better to know it was nothing personal.

"Forget it," Jeremy said. "No need to chase me out of here. I'll go."

"Don't come back."

Jeremy had no reason to ever come back. He'd only come to see Frank. It was Friday, and after work on Friday, he was sure, if it were possible to predict anything anymore, Frank would go to the pub around the corner. Jeremy would wait for him there, at the Eight Ball Saloon. And then he would put Dubasky and Cohen and its building's visitation policies behind him, forever.

Chapter 17

A billiards eight ball was painted on the storefront window, with a green shamrock in place of the 8. The Eight Ball Saloon had in its darkened interior four pool tables and, in the corner to the left of the entrance, a Foosball table, with rows of six-inch tall red and green plastic soccer players pierced through their sides by thin chrome poles. The goalie for the red team was missing his head, and the Eight Ball's wood floors were in need of a good waxing, but the beer was cheap and the pretzels free. A bar with brass railings ran the length of the establishment, with glasses hanging from overhead racks and against the wall bottles of every shape and size backed by smoked mirrors. Jeremy sat at the bar on a wood stool and ordered a draft beer.

"ID?" the bartender asked. He was Irish, short, with blue eyes, a thin mustache, and dirty blond hair, and had been serving drinks at the Eight Ball Saloon since before Jeremy first started working for Dubasky and Cohen.

"ID? Dan, it's me, Jeremy."

"Am I supposed to know you?" the bartender asked.

"I only came here for seven years," Jeremy said. "With my friend, Frank, from around the corner."

"I know Frank all right, but I don't know you. A lot of people come in here every week. I can't remember all of them." There were two other men sitting on stools and at a table near the back a group of three, a man and two women, smoking cigarettes and laughing.

He tried not to let the bartender's poor memory bother him. Jeremy was getting on with his own life, and Dan the bartender had apparently gotten on with his. "Oh well, I guess I haven't been here in a while. It's nice to see the place hasn't changed. It's perfect just the way it is."

"It's paradise," the bartender said. "You got ID?"

Jeremy showed his identification. He supposed being asked to prove that he was old enough to have a beer was at this late date a compliment, if an unintended one. The beer was cold. Jeremy wasn't a big drinker, had never been— he'd lived at home with his mother while attending college, and late night reruns of bad movies were the closest he'd come to experiencing animal house parties—but the occasional beer or two gave him nothing but pleasure. He drank slowly. The half mug of his remaining beer was not yet warm when Frank entered the bar.

Frank hung his royal blue ski coat on a hook on the wall, behind the Foosball table. Over a white mock turtleneck he wore his green vest with its many pockets. Frank reminded Jeremy of a man on safari—he just needed one of those hats, the ones from old Tarzan movies worn by English-speaking white men, confident in the superiority of their culture and their guns and full of arrogance, until the guileless natives kill them. With his vest and his swagger he was an everyday Han Solo—a rogue, a man with adventure in his heart. He didn't notice Jeremy when he came to the bar and got a pitcher of beer, and returned to the Foosball table without saying a word.

Jeremy walked to the Foosball table. Frank's back was to him, and Jeremy was about to speak when a voice came from the entrance.

"Frank," a young man said as he opened the door and entered the Eight Ball Saloon. He was lean and tall, with black hair and a nose that ended with an abrupt point. Draped in a large red sweater, he seemed small—his hands were almost hidden.

Frank turned. "Keith, where the hell you been?"

"There were some last minute packages going out," the young man named Keith said.

"Get some quarters," Frank said. Keith went to the bar.

"Hello, Frank," Jeremy said.

Frank shifted his head to the left and for the first time saw Jeremy, standing just a few feet away.

"How are you?" Jeremy asked.

Frank said nothing. His mouth was open.

"Frank, are you OK?" Jeremy asked.

Frank stared dumbly for a few more seconds. "Jeremy, what are you doing here?"

"I came to see you," Jeremy said. "I thought we should talk."

Keith returned with a handful of quarters.

"Jeremy, this is Keith. Keith, Jeremy. I have to go to the bathroom," Frank said, and he rushed to the back, past the CD jukebox, and around the corner to the restrooms.

Soon I'll be in charge of selling flaps to planes making international flights."

"Only international?" Frank asked.

"For starters," Jeremy said. "It's a very complicated business."

"It doesn't sound complicated," Keith said.

"You obviously know very little about aerodynamics," Jeremy said.

Keith said nothing.

"Without flaps, planes wouldn't be able to slow down or land. If not for people like me selling the right kind of flaps to airplane manufacturers, thousands of planes would be stuck flying around forever, with no way to land. It's sensitive and demanding work. You can't have flaps intended for international planes ending up on the wings of domestic flights. It would be tragic. Why do you think planes are falling out of the sky? People aren't paying enough attention to the flaps."

"I had no idea," Keith said.

"So," Frank said, stepping between Keith and Jeremy, "what brings you here?"

"Well," Jeremy said, "I wanted to talk to you." He placed his empty beer mug on the Foosball table.

"About what?"

Jeremy had it all worked out in his mind. He would tell Frank that in the first place he wasn't responsible for the unfortunate incident and Claude's injury, that misunderstandings happen and no one should lose his job because of it, that he had done nothing but work his heart out for the mailroom, been only the most devoted employee he knew how to be for seven years. He would add that friendship and loyalty were not things to be taken lightly, and he would ask Frank how he could possibly forget the time they had worked together as if it meant nothing. He worked himself up to an internal frenzy, gathering his thoughts and trying to find before he spoke the right words to express them. As he was about to let it all out in a moment of unbridled fury in the name of unrequited justice, he backed into the Foosball table, knocking his beer mug off the edge. It fell with extraordinary patience, as if winking at Jeremy and daring him to try to catch it. He could only stand helpless as the glass mug smashed to pieces on the floor.

"Hey, buddy," the bartender yelled. "Take it easy."

Jeremy knelt and picked up the largest piece of broken glass, a jagged edge connected to the mug's handle, hoping that cleaning the mess would appease Dan the bartender.

"Stay right there," a man in the front doorway said. It was Detective Jackson. The setting sun made his bald head shine. He was pointing his gun, a handful of black snubnosed destruction, at Jeremy. "Put down the glass. Slowly."

"I'm just picking up the—"

"—I didn't say you could speak," Detective Jackson said. "Put down the glass."

Jeremy heard the gun click in preparation for firing, and let the remnant of the shattered mug fall to the floor, where it clinked in protest.

"Good," Detective Jackson said. "Now move away, and keep your hands where I can see 'em."

Jeremy followed his instructions.

"Did he hurt either of you?" Detective Jackson asked Frank and Keith.

"No," Frank said.

"Then I got here in the nick of time," Detective Jackson said.

"Actually," Frank said, "he didn't break the mug to use as a weapon against us. It fell and broke by accident."

"Are you certain?" Detective Jackson asked.

"Yes," Frank said.

"I guess you can put your hands down," Detective Jackson said to Jeremy.

Jeremy kept his hands in the air. Nothing, not on the subway platform or in the Korean grocery or earlier today with the woman defending her car with hydrochloric acid, nothing compared to having a gun pointed at him.

"I said you can put your hands down," Detective Jackson said, holstering his weapon beneath his gray sport coat.

Jeremy lowered his arms, but stayed against the wall.

"I don't think he meant us any harm," Frank said, ignoring Jeremy in the way adults had of talking in a child's presence as if the child were too simple to understand that it was the subject of their words.

"You have no idea what he's capable of," Detective Jackson said to Frank. "You were right to call me."

Jeremy should have known. He had made the mistake of trusting Frank, but trust and betrayal were cut from the same cloth.

"You said I should if he came back," Frank said. He was flush with the energy of the moment, full of the possibilities of a drawn gun, broken glass, standing up straighter with pride at his own composure and, yes, even heroism, in the face of danger.

"You should go now," Detective Jackson said to Frank and Keith. "This is a police matter."

"Is there anything else you need from me?" Frank asked the detective, eager to be a part of the continuing excitement.

"You've done a fine job," Detective Jackson said, "but I

have it from here."

Without looking at Jeremy or saying another word Frank and Keith exited the Eight Ball Saloon.

"Did you think you were going to get away with it?" Detective Jackson asked.

"Get away with what?" Jeremy asked.

"Don't play dumb with me," Detective Jackson said.

"I'm not playing. I don't know what you're talking about."

"You went to Dubasky and Cohen and then you came here," Detective Jackson said. "You can't hide anything from me."

"Who's hiding anything?"

"So you did go to Dubasky and Cohen. I knew it."

"Yeah, to see my friends. People I thought were friends," Jeremy said.

"Well, it was your last visit. I don't want to hear that you went to Dubasky and Cohen again."

"I can go anywhere I want."

"You can't go there."

"It's a free country. I'm a free man. I'll go wherever it pleases me to go."

"You are so naive," Detective Jackson said, removing an envelope from his jacket pocket and handing it to Jeremy.

"What's this?"

"That, my friend, is a restraining order. If you come within one hundred yards of the building you used to work in, or fifty yards of anyone who works in the building or for any of Dubasky and Cohen's vendors or clients, you will be arrested for violation of the restraining order."

"You can't do this," Jeremy said.

"I can and I have," Detective Jackson said.

"What if I'm within fifty yards of someone who works

in the building, but I don't know they work in the building? Will I go to jail?"

"Don't use your crazy logic on me."

"I just want to know—"

"—I've had enough of you," Detective Jackson said. "Now make yourself scarce."

"I don't plan on ever coming back anyway."

"You'd better not. If you do, I'll be on you like white on rice."

"Have you ever listened to yourself talk?" Jeremy asked. "You sound like a movie, or a TV show."

"I sound just fine," Detective Jackson said. "I'm not the one planting bombs in buildings. I'm not the one mugging people. Or raping them. I keep the streets safe from people like you. I protect the innocent. I'm the backbone of our civilization, the fabric of our society. You're something people scrape off the bottom of their shoes. Don't forget it."

"I'll bear it in mind," Jeremy said, walking to the door. Then, in his most pleasant voice, he said, "Have a nice day." Jeremy didn't have a gun, or any other weapon, but wished, if only for a second, that it really were possible to kill someone with kindness.

Chapter 18

Going to see Frank was a mistake. Jeremy knew that now. Not because of the overzealous Detective Jackson, but because it wasn't Frank Jeremy needed to see in order to put his past behind him. It was Claude. If Jeremy had done wrong to anyone, if he bore responsibility for a fraction of the misery in any soul other than his own, it was Claude's. It was the image of Claude leaning against a powder blue wall, with blood winding its way from his wrist, that visited Jeremy in the dark when sleep didn't answer his call. He'd made moral sense of most of it, of the world's seeming grudge against him, of the anger he couldn't avoid bumping into in his effort to live, but the memory of Claude's blind stare and silent pain were roadblocks to the peace of mind he desired before finally fulfilling his destiny.

Rationalization was a broad weapon, like a machine gun cutting down all obstacles in its sights. Jeremy had sprayed bullets of logic to excuse the offenses committed by the grocer and his fork, the twelve-year-old mugger on the subway, the security guard with the tattoo, shot in his own forgiving conscience hundreds of rounds at the acid queen and her foreign car with the polite but firm speaking voice, at Frank, even emptied a clip in the direction of Detective Jackson. They all had jobs to do, all faced pressures imposed on them by the world, weren't bad people and in their hearts meant him no harm. If their actions were harsh or uncaring, it wasn't a reflection of the truest parts of themselves. Judgments were hard to make, and words like good and evil didn't seem to apply. He liked instead the word troubled. Everyone was troubled, and if people weren't marionettes, mere slaves to circumstance, they weren't quite Pinnochio either, freed by a fairy from the strings of fate and made alive. Jeremy fired forgiveness at all of them. But he couldn't turn the rifle of rationalization on himself—his guilt had its own instinct for survival, and kept him from pulling the trigger.

There could be no joy in the culmination of his adventure, in the realization of his destiny, without first making things right with Claude. Jeremy couldn't sleep another night until he'd seen with his own eyes that Claude was not as bad off as Frank had said. He rested a couple of hours after leaving the Eight Ball Saloon, ate a few peanut butter and jelly sandwiches for the energy to see his mission through, and caught the train leaving Penn Station for Long Island twenty minutes after nine. Jeremy had found in the beat-up desk adjacent to the kitchenette in his studio apartment a list with the addresses and phone numbers of Dubasky and Cohen's mailroom employees. He remembered the list, but wasn't sure that he still had it until searching and finding it buried by 2,918 filthy rubber bands. The list was a few years old, and contained the names of twelve people who had been let go before Jeremy's career met its own untimely end. Jeremy tried not to think that an updated list posted somewhere in the mailroom had Keith's name in place of his own.

The Long Island Railroad was usually as busy as the Manhattan subway, but it was late Friday, and rush hour had ended. A few scattered souls were on Jeremy's car. Drinks were sold on the railroad platform, a privilege reserved for those leaving Manhattan at the close of the workweek. The departing cocktail or beer was to them the same as a decompression chamber was to a scuba diver. Without it there was little hope of recovering from a too long stay beneath the ocean's depths. The drinks were expensive, like on an airplane, but many in the captive audience gladly paid. The little drink stand and the polite man serving them were not to be taken for granted—people riding buses or the subway home had no such luxury, and the gears of the illusion that the pressures of life could be left behind in the city demanded a persuasive lubricant.

The train rattled on. Jeremy's seat faced the wrong way—the train did not turn around at the end of a trip, but simply headed in the opposite direction, its front becoming its back, and its back becoming its front. All Jeremy could see through the window was where the train had just been, not where it was going. After a few minutes he changed his seat, and felt more relaxed now that he could see the dead trees and vacant lots and smoking stacks before the train had already passed them. It wasn't a long trip, maybe totaling a half-hour until the Great Neck stop, not far from where Claude lived with his parents. Jeremy didn't know exactly what he would say, what reason he could give for being at their home, but tried not to worry about it. The anticipation of seeing Claude and freeing himself from his past overshadowed all else.

More than halfway there, just after the Bayside stop, an older black man with gray hair came onto the car through the connecting door from the car behind it, wearing no coat and only red sneakers, green slacks, and a yellow sweater. His clothes were clean and his shoes new. He walked swiftly and stared at the floor as he moved, halting when he reached the middle of the car. "There they are," he said, pointing at the floor, then yelled, "There they are! Right there!"

Jeremy was seated three rows from the middle of the car, and turned his head and leaned to get a better look at the object of this great concern. He saw nothing but the white floor, a little dirty, with a piece of gum ground into it and old scuffmarks. Nothing out of the ordinary.

"They're coming up! I can't stop them!" the man yelled. One of his eyes wandered, independent of the other, which managed to stay focused on the same spot on the floor of the train. He turned and backed toward Jeremy's section, never letting his good eye leave the spot on the floor. Jeremy still saw nothing interesting there, but the man held his hands out as if trying to prevent whatever he saw on the floor from getting any closer. He must have been seventy. His physique indicated a slightly younger man, but his eyes were old. Something in his unchanging expression and the locked half of his gaze added years, told the world that whatever was chasing him from somewhere deep in the floor was winning, was wearing him out.

The older man became aware of the people around him, of Jeremy and another, a white man, close to forty, in wool slacks and with a potbelly not quite hidden by his cashmere sweater and leather jacket. The older man turned from the spot on the floor, and said in a single rushed breath, "They're coming help they're here!" Once the last word was spoken his attention returned to the floor.

Jeremy looked at the floor but still saw nothing. The fear in the man's voice was real, and Jeremy tried to comfort him. "There's nothing there. No one's going to hurt you."

The older man didn't seem to hear the words, and walked back to the middle of the car, again standing over the same area and staring at the floor. "Save me!" he screamed. "They're getting me!" He flailed his arms at nothing and shrieked, echoing throughout the car his awful pain.

"There's nothing there," Jeremy said.

The older man ceased his flailing and shrieking and rushed in his clumsy and determined fashion back to the seats near Jeremy. "Save me!" he pleaded. He spoke not to Jeremy but to the man sitting in the next row, in the sweater and leather jacket.

The man ignored this nonsense, and tried to finish his martini and read his automobile magazine with a Rolls Royce on the cover.

"Save me!" the older black man yelled.

The man in the leather jacket turned his page. His recently manicured fingernails shined with clear polish.

"They're right here!" the older man said, sticking his face up against the cover of the automobile magazine.

"I can't help you," the man with the magazine said, looking straight ahead.

"They're climbing on me!" the older man said, and he shook his arm to free himself of whatever he saw crawling up his yellow sleeve. In his panicked thrashing he knocked the magazine from the man's hand.

"What the hell you think you're doing?" the man in the

leather jacket asked. He reached down to retrieve his reading material, but the older man stomped on the magazine with his new sneakers.

"I got them!" he yelled. "I got them!" And the panic disappeared from his voice. One planted sneaker held the magazine in place as the other ripped its cover in half. He stomped on the magazine twice more and then walked back to the middle of the train, cackling almost to himself, but looking with concern again at the same spot on the floor. The older man saw nothing funny there, and his laughter left him. "This isn't good," he said.

The man removed his leather jacket, set his cup on his seat, and walked to the middle of the train. "Hey, pal, you owe me one issue of *Tires And Buyers*," he said to the old man.

The older black man in the yellow sweater clutched at his own throat and made a gurgling sound. "They're choking me!" he said, pushing the words out with a gasp.

"Hey," the man no longer wearing a leather jacket said, "I'm talking to you. That magazine cost me three bucks."

"They're coming!" the older man said.

"I'm not kidding. That magazine was three bucks."

"Help me!" the older man cried, and he reached for the potbellied man.

The younger man moved aside with dexterity, his fat stomach bouncing. He raised his arms, one higher than the other, his hands each tight in the shape of a lobster claw, and inched his foot forward. "I know karate," he warned.

"They're all over me!" the older man yelled, trying to brush the unseen invaders from his chest and shoulders. He twisted and turned in his attempt to swipe the creatures from his back, like a dog chasing its tail.

The man maintained his karate attack posture. "Give me the money for the magazine." He was ready to fight, bobbing his head as if preparing to dodge blows.

"Leave him alone," Jeremy said to the man with the potbelly and the Kung Fu grip.

"Stay out of this," the man said, then to the older man, "Your act doesn't cut it with me."

"That's no act," Jeremy said.

"Fall for it if you want," the man said, "but I won't. He just wants sympathy. He ruined my magazine, and I want compensation."

"Are you insane?" Jeremy asked.

"We can't let them push us around," the man said. "No matter how many of us they shoot down on the trains, no matter how many riots and tantrums they throw."

The older man smacked himself in the face and growled. He punched the air to his left, his arms a whirling windmill, as if his demons were real and standing before him.

"Howl all you want," the karate man said. "Your black rage doesn't scare me. I have white rage. I'll kick you right in the teeth. I've been training for four years because of people like you."

"I'll give you the three dollars," Jeremy said.

"I don't want your money. This isn't about that," the man said.

"Take it," Jeremy said. "You don't need to kick his teeth out. Buy yourself another magazine."

"This is about justice. About payback," the man said.

"Here's three dollars. Don't hurt him. He's sick. Please," Jeremy said.

"Let me see it," the man said, keeping a threatening bend

in his knees, ready to let fly with a country club karate kick, if necessary.

Jeremy held up three crumpled dollars.

"I want new bills," the man said, gesturing with one hand-lobster-claw, his eyes alive with menace.

"I don't have new ones," Jeremy said.

"I want new ones."

"What are you going to do? Beat up this old man? He doesn't have money. I do. Just take it and forget the whole thing."

Before the karate man could answer, the older man screamed in greater agony than before, scratching at himself in desperation.

"It's OK," Jeremy told him. "I won't let them hurt you."

Nothing said could penetrate the older man's torture. He groaned with his suffering, pulling at his own hair and throwing himself against the closed train exit. He fell to the floor and rolled around, as a man on fire.

The potbellied man jumped out of the way.

"They're getting me!" the older man cried, tears covering his face. Then he stopped crying and beating himself, and stood up with an unexpected spring. "Where are they?" he asked, examining the floor as if it had answers for him, and as suddenly as he had entered their train he departed, walking through the connecting door to the car ahead of this one.

Jeremy and the man next to him were both silent. There weren't words to make sense of it. Jeremy thought about following the older man, but didn't know what he could do to help. The conductor was in the next car—Jeremy could see him watching the crazy old man. It was the conductor's train—he would have to call the police; they would return this lost soul to whatever institution had carelessly left its doors open. Jeremy had done all he could, all he had the stomach for. Sometimes he thought he was a lightning rod for all suffering; a conduit for torments real and imagined and not always his own ran into him from all directions and charged him with its emotional electricity. It was too great a burden, and Jeremy wanted more than anything to be free of it. The man and his lunacy made Jeremy think of Claude. If he were in any way responsible for causing this kind of pain in poor, innocent Claude, he could never forgive himself.

"Excuse me," the potbellied man said, calm now that the older crazy man was gone. He snatched the three dollars from Jeremy's hand, and said, "I believe these are mine."

Jeremy didn't bother arguing with the middle-aged karate kid, and chalked up the three dollars as a donation to benefit all those misplaced and maladjusted riders of trains without destinations. He needed to save his energy for seeing Claude, and the three dollars were insignificant in light of his new job. Most of all, life was too short to instigate a fight with Long Island lobster-claw.

Chapter 19

With only an address to guide him the driver of the dark car was on his way to Claude's house. The private taxi company had a dozen sedans waiting at the train station—yellow cabs rarely ventured far from the city, and the closer one got to Long Island the more often these four-door leftovers from late night reruns of *The A-Team* doubled as taxis. These cabs had no meters, and charged a flat fee based on the distance of the trip. The driver checked in with his dispatcher on the CB—Jeremy's fare would be six dollars. The car wound its way up hills, pine trees all around, and passed homes one after the other with long, snaking driveways and basketball hoops in front of two-car garages and thick hedges to prevent uninvited scrutiny.

"You must know every address in Great Neck," Jeremy said with admiration to the driver. Knowing how to get around the city was one thing—most of Manhattan was a grid and easy to navigate, with numbered streets and avenues—but finding an address here, where Flower Lanes and Peach Tree Drives and Daffodil Places and Possum Boulevards crossed and twisted without regard or consideration for wandering travelers, was a skill to be prized and praised.

"I know these hills like the back of my hand," the driver said. He was huge, with brown hair parted on the right side. The top of his head rubbed the car's ceiling. Being familiar with the back roads, he said, with the ins and outs of all of the island, was essential. When it all came down his knowledge would prove its value—his family's survival might depend on it.

"When what all comes down?" Jeremy asked. If there were a cataclysmic event on the immediate horizon he wanted to know about it.

"You can never tell," the driver said. "It might be anything. I have my suspicions, but I can't be sure about the specifics. You can bet something will happen, though.

"Is the world going to explode or something?" Jeremy asked.

"We mock what we don't understand."

"I'm not mocking you."

"It sounds like mockery to me," the driver said.

"I didn't mean it. I just haven't heard of any impending disaster. Wouldn't there have been some announcement if anything was wrong?"

"What if the disaster is caused by the very authority you hope will warn you?" the driver asked, a question it was obvious to Jeremy he'd asked before.

"Is this one of those conspiracy theories?" Jeremy asked.

"This isn't a theory, or small-town gossip, or paranoia. There's documentation."

"About what?"

"The government. The government," the driver said. "They can't be trusted."

"Can you trust anyone these days?" Jeremy asked, immediately disappointed with his own cynicism.

"If you know how to spot the enemy you can. We've banded together, some of us. To protect our freedom. It's a brotherhood, a strong one. We used to communicate on the shortwave, but now we have the Internet. It's our best weapon. It may be humanity's last hope."

"You think someone is trying to take away your freedom?"

"I don't think. I know they are. Did you know that in the sixties and seventies our government injected its citizens—this happened to Americans, here, in the land of the free—they injected them with plutonium and uranium. Did you know that?"

"No," Jeremy said.

"This isn't the raving of a lunatic—I'm not making this stuff up. It was in the *New York Times*. But even they were fooled. Or probably they're in on it too. Either way, they failed to report the true significance of the government's plan. They said the injections were to test human reaction to radiation, in case there was a nuclear war or meltdown."

"It wasn't?"

"I know the truth. The awful truth," he said. "The government's been cloning sheep and monkeys for years, for decades."

"I thought it was a recent breakthrough."

"That's what they want you to think," the driver said.

"How do you know all this?"

"I have my sources."

"Anyway, I don't see the connection," Jeremy said.

"Of course you don't. You've been brainwashed, like the

rest of the country. By the liberal media, by the powers who don't want you to know the truth."

"I don't feel brainwashed."

"You wouldn't *be* brainwashed if you felt brainwashed," the driver said. "Denial is the first sign. It's the people who think they're free who never are."

"So," Jeremy said, a little insulted, "if me and my feeble mind can ask, what's the government's plan?"

"Don't you see? It's as clear as a child's lesson book. They're building a master race. With radiation and cloning they're making perfect people. People who won't challenge them, won't ask any questions. They're making an army. When they have enough irradiated clones the war will begin. But we'll be ready. We have our Geiger counters—we can detect their operatives. And we have weapons of our own."

"You believe all this?"

"Don't try to make me sound like the crazy one," the driver said. "The government made sure to first announce the cloning of the sheep. Our enemy is fond of symbolism—you're all sheep, being herded toward destruction. The answers are there, for all to see, if you open your eyes."

"How do you know I'm not one of them?"

"I tested you when you got in the car. I have a Geiger counter in the front seat. If you were one of them it would have alerted me."

"And what would've you done?" Jeremy asked.

"If you were a radiation clone?"

"Yeah, if I was a radiation clone."

"I'd have unloaded my nine millimeter into you. Then I would've replaced the clip, and unloaded that into you too."

"I'm glad your Geiger counter is working properly," Jeremy said. "You're armed, now?"

"Don't worry," the driver said. "I wouldn't shoot you. Us humans have to stick together."

They arrived at Claude's house, and Jeremy paid his six-dollar fare and gave a two-dollar tip. "For the cause," he told the driver, relieved a moment later to see the car's taillights disappear around a dark corner.

Jeremy walked up the steep blacktop driveway. Though only a few miles removed from shops and main roads, the house seemed isolated in the still night air. Thick trees and bushes created the happy illusion of privacy—nearby houses couldn't be seen. A mailbox on a wood pole completed the picture of serene country life. Jeremy thought that here, away from overflowing trains and congested sidewalks, from honking cars and emergency sirens, from the inevitable madness that resulted when ten million people breathed the same stagnant oxygen, was the peaceful existence he craved. Waking to a cicada's longing calls instead of the cranky sanitation truck's jaws crushing garbage, smelling the morning dew on a forest breeze and not the fumes of the city bus that had a schedule to keep, was, Jeremy was sure, an antidote for all wrongs, for every slight.

The two-story white house had octagonal columns supporting a railed-in balcony. On the front lawn was a wood bench hanging from chains around an oak's thick branch. Claude was lucky. Whatever pressures had sent him to that bathroom and compelled him to slice himself with a broken mirror couldn't have followed him here. Stress of any kind couldn't survive a single relaxing swing on that wood bench hanging from a tree. This is where Claude belonged. Jeremy had doubts about the competence of parents who would send their retarded son out from this paradise to the hustle and bustle of life in the big city. What could the city give him that couldn't be found here? Claude didn't dine at expensive restaurants or go to Broadway shows or take in the occasional opera. Jeremy guessed that getting him out of the house, gaining freedom from his neediness, had been a prime motivation in his employment at Dubasky and Cohen.

There was no doorbell, only a shining golden knocker with a carved gargoyle's face. Jeremy knocked. No one answered the door. He knocked again, slamming the gargoyle three times, but still got no response from inside the house. He looked through a window to the left of the door. The lights were on, so somebody had to be home. Jeremy knocked again. Nothing. He tested the doorknob and was surprised when it turned. The door wasn't locked. Doors in Manhattan were never left unlocked. It was rare if a front door wasn't double locked and chained. Things were different out here. There was less crime—who would drive up and around these hills just to rob a house? But Jeremy didn't think it was a great idea not to lock doors, even this far from the dangerous city. Some maniac could walk right in without any warning.

He opened the door and shouted, "Hello? Is anybody home?" He didn't want to be mistaken for a burglar.

No one replied. The house's wood floors were shining where they weren't covered by plush red rugs with oriental designs. To the left was a small room with a rocking chair and a loveseat, and to the right a larger room with a brick fireplace, and two couches, covered by fine, textured fabric, encircling a glass coffee table. A painting of a woman, in a brass frame like the kind Jeremy had seen as a kid on school trips to the Metropolitan Museum of Art, was above the mantle. She looked like the Queen of England, with black, sculpted hair, pale skin, and a stern expression. The stairs to the second floor were visible from the doorway, and Jeremy ascended. "Is anyone here?" he asked.

The house's walls were barren—not a single photograph or painting except for the one downstairs over the mantle. The first room on the right was filled with closed cardboard boxes. Up ahead and to the left was another room with an open door. Jeremy asked again, "Is anyone here?" In this room on the left was Claude, tucked into his bed tight, his arms not showing from beneath the Spiderman blanket. His eyes were open and he was staring at the ceiling. A television sat on a small dresser and there was a blue beanbag in the corner of the room. Claude didn't look bad, and Jeremy was happy to note that he was no thinner than he had been when they worked together.

"Claude, it's me, Jeremy."

Claude continued examining the ceiling.

"Claude, can you hear me?"

Claude did nothing to indicate he was aware of Jeremy's presence.

"I don't know if you understand me," Jeremy said, standing now at the foot of the single bed, "but I came to visit because I wanted to see you, to make sure you were feeling good. Are you?"

Claude blinked, but Jeremy did not interpret this as an answer.

"Claude, I just want to tell you that I'm sorry—" Jeremy didn't finish the sentence, but fell to the carpeted floor, a sharp pain in his side.

"Who the hell are you?" Standing over Jeremy was a short man with black hair, speckled with gray. He was holding a golf club, a sand wedge, as if it were a baseball bat.

Jeremy had lost his wind from the unexpected blow, and was only able to cough in reply.

"Speak up," the man said. He was wearing a maroon bathrobe and black slippers and was a bit taller than Claude, still shorter than average.

"I'm not a thief," Jeremy was able to say in short forced breaths.

"No sudden movements," he said, still prepared to deliver a second blow with the golf club. "Who are you?"

"I used to work with Claude. I just came to visit him."

The man wasn't convinced. "How do you know his name?"

"I'm telling the truth. We worked together, at Dubasky and Cohen. You sit on the board."

"Why would you sneak in here?" the man asked.

"I knocked but no one answered," Jeremy said.

"That doesn't give you the right to break into someone's house."

"I'm sorry about that," Jeremy said, breathing a little easier, "but it was a long trip out here. I kept shouting but no one answered."

"I had drops in my ears," Claude's father said.

"I worked with Claude. I wouldn't lie about something like that."

Claude's father considered Jeremy for a moment, and looked him in the eye. "You have an honest face," he said.

"I'm sincere," Jeremy said. "I really didn't mean to scare you, but I was worried about how Claude was doing. How is he?"

"What you see is what you get. He just lies there."

"Does he always go to bed this early?" Jeremy asked, standing up.

"You don't understand," Claude's father said. "He just lies there. All the time. In the morning, all day. He spends his life staring at the ceiling. He doesn't even close his eyes when he sleeps at night. I shut them for him, the way you have to close a dead man's eyes. I don't know what he's looking at."

"How did this happen?"

"His mother, God rest her soul, she gave birth to him backwards."

"But he wasn't like this at work," Jeremy said. "He stuffed envelopes and took the train. He loved to look at the Empire State Building."

"He was doing well. After his mother died I didn't know what I would do with him. He took to that job, was able to look after himself. Not entirely, but more than before. But one day he lost it. I'm sure you heard the story. Someone screamed at him, because he was too slow or dumb, and he just lost it. He's been like this ever since."

"I'm sure there's something the doctors can do. They have very advanced techniques these days."

"They can't do anything," Claude's father said. "We've been to every specialist. I never should have let him go. He should have been here with me. Now he lies there all day, useless."

"But there are new experimental programs," Jeremy said. "There have to be. No one has to suffer like this anymore."

"There's nothing," Claude's father said. "My boy can't even feed himself. He can't talk, doesn't get up to go to the bathroom."

"Isn't there anything we can do for him?"

Claude's father spoke in a whisper and held back tears. "My boy wears a diaper. I never changed his diaper when he was a baby. His mother took care of that. He's twenty-six years old and now I finally get to change his diaper. My boy's twenty-six and can't wipe his own ass."

"There must be something."

"Nothing," Claude's father said through his light, hiccuping sobs.

"I don't believe it."

"This is how it is. This is how it is for us now."

"It doesn't have to be this way. There's got to be something."

"There's nothing."

"It doesn't have to be like this," Jeremy said, almost to himself.

"There's nothing. This is how it is for us now."

Chapter 20

Monday's morning was full of possibilities. Jeremy recalled a bumper sticker he'd seen on a truck on the turnpike, years earlier on his way to visit cousins in New Jersey: *Today is the first day of the rest of your life.* The truck was delivering milk and had Wisconsin plates. Maybe it was possible for that truck driver to start over with each new sun. Road and more road always beckoned, and whatever troubles the truck driver was fleeing by staying up all night so people in Bergen or New Haven could have fresh milk might well be banished by the blasting music and the spinning wheels and the knowledge that if the past gave chase the highway ahead was open. But Jeremy's own past had turned out not to be as fickle as he had hoped. Even as time marched on and the world quickly forgot the way things once were he remained stuck with his own history, unable to escape it any more than he could escape his skin.

Claude's father couldn't escape his own skin either, and Claude was himself trapped by some unnamed horror. An adventure on Long Island hadn't granted Jeremy a clean slate, but slates were hard to cleanse—maybe they were dirty from the outset. He couldn't make sense of Claude, of his suffering and his silence, couldn't abdicate his own responsibility for Claude's inner paralysis. Jeremy wouldn't be able to simply start over—yesterday had power over today, and tomorrow too. But Monday didn't care for yesterdays, and dangled possibility like a carrot—with a new job and the promise of a revelatory meeting with the man with the bushy mustache. Poor Claude would always be there, in some recess of Jeremy's mind, visiting without warning to remind him that he had caused suffering in this world. Still, it was Monday, and Jeremy's highway was clear and smooth before him.

His new job, in addition to whatever advantages he was certain it would provide, was an easy commute. Just three stops downtown on the subway. The people were shoulder to shoulder, all reaching for balance to handles on chrome poles along the ceiling. They were mostly silent, as if trying to gather energy for the coming week.

"People, hear me," a black woman in a large pink hat said. She was the same woman he had seen so many mornings reading aloud from her Bible and being ignored. It had been maybe half a year since she'd made an appearance, as far as Jeremy knew, and she made him think of the homeless man with the Swiss cheese sneakers who used to sing *Strangers in the Night*. There was no sign of the man with the deep voice. But the woman was there, and read from her creased black book with passion. Jeremy didn't know how she saw the tiny print, but she read without stumbling in an escalating rhythm.

"Cut down the trees and build siege ramps against Jerusalem. This city must be punished; it is filled with oppression. As a well pours out its water, so she pours out her wickedness. Violence and destruction resound in her; her sickness and wounds are ever before me. Take warning, O Jerusalem, or I will turn away from you and make your land desolate so no one can live in it."

"Will you please shut up with that nonsense?" a man sitting near the woman said. He was in a suit and was tapping his brown briefcase with his thumbs.

"Excuse me?" the woman asked, assuming her ears had deceived her.

"I asked if you could please shut up. No one wants to hear about how evil we are," the man said.

The dozens of people on their train car said nothing. Subway preaching, though not as common as it once was, hardly qualified as worth attention. Only the man's response, his decision to confront the woman and her Bible, interested the drained passengers preparing for another day.

The woman stared at her challenger and read louder and more fervently. "Stand at the crossroads and look; ask for the ancient paths, ask where the good way is and walk in it, and you will find rest for your souls. But you said 'We will not walk in it.' I appointed watchmen over you and said, 'Listen to the sound of the trumpet!' But you said, 'We will not listen.'"

"Babble all you want," the man who still played drums on his briefcase said. "You can't change anything. These people are on their way to work. They're doing something with their lives. They don't have time for you."

The woman didn't answer him but read even louder, making herself heard throughout the car. "I am bringing disaster on this people, the fruit of their schemes, because they have not listened to my words and have rejected my law. What do I care about incense from Sheba or sweet calamus from a distant land? Your burnt offerings are not acceptable; your sacrifices do not please me."

Jeremy's stop came before the man could answer the woman's divine accusations and threats. The problem with people, he thought, the reason so many of them preached or balked at being preached to, was that they lacked direction, a purpose in life. And they were alone. Jeremy was fortunate to be beginning a new career, to have a destiny, and to have a caring woman in his future. Though he hadn't spoken to Brooke since their date, had been busy and more to the point had avoided Strawberry Dreams for fear that she would be angry at him for not telling her the truth about his allergy, Jeremy knew in his heart she would forgive him. After he discovered his destiny and met with the man with the bushy mustache, Jeremy would visit Brooke at Strawberry Dreams. Then he would be complete, a man with a career, an exalted, purposeful life, and a woman who loved him.

He arrived at the office building for his new job, before nine and wearing a tie, as his brother had instructed, to find a picket line blocking his way. Three women and two men, all white, looking like kids, maybe old enough to be in college, held signs and paced. They chanted in unison: "Fur is murder. Fur is murder." The five signs were hand-painted: *Animals Are People Too* and *Save Our Furry Friends* and *Don't Be A Fur-Wearing Jerk* and *Fur is Bad* and *Don't Wear Them, Hug Them.*

When Jeremy tried to walk past the protesters, their leader, a woman with green hair and a nose ring and black lipstick, blocked his way. "You can't go in there," she said.

"Why not?" Jeremy asked.

"This building houses an evil corporation," she said.

Jeremy pulled out the business card Marc had given him and said, "There are a lot of companies in this building. I work for RGP. Are they the evil corporation?"

"No," she said. "Not specifically. But I would bet they do evil."

"I don't know anything about them," Jeremy said. "Today's my first day. But I don't have any reason to suspect that RGP is any more evil than any other company."

"They're all evil. The capitalist swine. Keeping the people down."

"I'm sure that RGP is better than that."

"How can you stand to work for the man?"

Jeremy wasn't quite sure who the man was. He'd never heard white people use the term before. "I've got rent to pay. How do you get your money?"

"Money is the root of all evil," she said.

"Maybe it is," Jeremy said. "But the rent doesn't pay itself. How do you do it without money?"

"I don't bother with it. I won't soil my hands."

"Do you live on the street?" Jeremy asked.

"No."

"And you don't have to pay rent?"

"No," she said. "My father has an apartment in SoHo he doesn't use."

"I really do have to go inside," Jeremy said.

"What about the poor animals?"

"They kill the animals here?" Jeremy didn't love the idea of being in the same building as a slaughterhouse.

"Not exactly. They make fake fur coats."

"You're protesting a company that makes fake fur coats?"

Jeremy asked, letting out a laugh.

"There's nothing funny about killing cute, cuddly animals. How would you like it if someone skinned you alive and made a coat out of you?"

"I wouldn't like that at all."

"Then join our protest."

"You're picketing a company that doesn't even use animals."

"But they make coats which look exactly like real fur," she said.

"So?"

"It sends the wrong message," she said.

"What message is it sending?"

"It objectifies animals. Like the way pornography debases women, these coats say it's OK to wear animals."

"I don't know," Jeremy said.

"Plus," she said, trying to convince him, "they're making a travesty of our anti-fur campaign. These furs look so real, we can't tell them apart from the authentic coats. Before you know it, no one will be able to tell them apart."

"That sounds like great news. Maybe the people who want to wear furs will instead start wearing these authentic fakes. Maybe this company will actually help stop the cruelty, and even the greatest fur supporters will stop killing animals."

"That would be terrible," she said.

"Why?"

She spoke to him with all the angst of one who has envisioned a future catastrophe but is powerless to prevent it. "If all the people stop wearing fur coats, how are we going to tell the good from the bad?"

Chapter 21

Just ten feet inside the building's front door was a security guard sitting behind a bridge table. He was an older man, with white hair and red cheeks. His walkie-talkie sitting on the table was tuned to a police channel: *We got a 187, that's a 1, 8, 7, at St. Marks...*

"Excuse me," Jeremy said. He didn't want to be late for his first day.

"Hold your horses," the guard said, but the police report had already ended. "Someone sure bit the dust on that one. What can I do for you?"

"I start work today for RGP," Jeremy said.

"What do you want, a medal?" the guard asked.

"I didn't know if I had to check in with you or anything."

The lobby had a high ceiling, with track lighting. An escalator and marble staircase rose to the second floor, where Jeremy could see four elevators waiting. A metal detector was to the guard's left, and wood barricades on the detector's other side to the wall prevented anyone from getting to the escalator or stairs without first passing through the weapon-sniffing arch.

"All you gotta do is pass through this metal detector. RGP is on the eighth floor."

"What do you have a metal detector for?" Jeremy asked.

"To detect metal," the guard said.

"I mean, why do you need a metal detector?"

"There have been bomb threats against the building. We think from anti-fur protesters. Besides, there are twenty-nine floors in this place, thirty-one separate companies. It's only a matter of time before we have a disgruntled employee try something rash."

"Why would you say that? Have there been any incidents?"

"Not yet," the guard said. "But you have to play the percentages. There are over eight hundred people working in this building, in some capacity or another. You can't find a random assortment of eight hundred people without a few loonies among them. Ten percent of the general population is insane."

"Ten percent?"

"Ten percent, maybe fifteen. And another ten percent are ready to go bonkers, are on the brink, if you will. Those are national figures, too. I would bet in New York the ratio is even higher."

"I didn't know that."

"You learn something new every day," the guard said, eager to return to the entertainment of the police channel. "All you have to do is go through the metal detector."

"Thanks," Jeremy said, and walked through the arch. It beeped.

"Take out your keys," the guard said.

Jeremy removed his keys and handed them to the guard.

He walked through, but the metal detector once more beeped.

The guard stood up. He had a revolver in a holster on one hip and handcuffs on the other. "You have any weapons on you?"

"No," Jeremy said.

"You don't have a gun or a knife, maybe a pocketknife or switchblade?"

"No. I don't have any weapons."

"Maybe it's your belt. The buckle is metal. Take it off."

Jeremy undid his belt and put it on the guard's table, then walked through the metal detector's arch. Beep.

"I don't understand," Jeremy said. "I don't have any metal on me."

"No subway tokens or jewelry?"

Jeremy emptied his pockets and removed his watch and his golden eagle with stretched wings and tried again. Still it beeped.

"Have you had any operations?" the guard asked. "Screws in your ankle or a steel plate in your head?"

"No."

"Are you sure?"

"I think I would know if I had a plate in my head."

"How else can you explain the beeping?" the guard asked.

"Maybe it's a malfunction."

"It isn't a malfunction."

"It could be."

The guard retrieved a handheld metal detector from a red bag under the bridge table. He ran it up and down Jeremy, front and back. It beeped as well. "Put your arms out," he said.

"Pardon me?"

"I need to frisk you for weapons."

"I don't have any," Jeremy said.

"We'll see about that."

"Your equipment is broken."

"One malfunction is possible," the guard said. "But two? I don't think so. Spread your arms."

"And if I say no?"

"Then you don't get in the building," the guard said.

Jeremy didn't want to be searched. He of course had no weapon, but considered this treatment a violation of his liberties. But his principles were secondary to the job waiting for him up on the eighth floor. He stretched his arms out and allowed the security guard to pat him down.

"Go on through," the guard said, after finding that Jeremy was telling the truth.

Jeremy retrieved his keys, belt, watch, and eagle. The escalator was not running. *Out of Order* was written on a piece of yellow paper and taped to the railing at the bottom. Jeremy reached the first step of the escalator when the guard yelled, "What are you doing?"

"I'm going upstairs to get an elevator," Jeremy said.

"Can you read?" the guard asked.

"Yes."

"What does that sign say?"

Jeremy stepped back down and looked at the piece of yellow paper. "Out of order," he said.

"Exactly," the guard said. "The escalator is out of order. Use the stairs."

"I was just going to walk up the escalator's steps."

"I know what you were going to do. I'm telling you that you can't."

"It doesn't matter to me if the escalator isn't running. I'll just walk up."

"Get off of that escalator and use the stairs."

"Why can't I just walk up the escalator?" A broken escalator was, after all, nothing more than metal steps.

"Insurance regulations," the guard told him.

"Insurance regulations?"

"Yes. If you get hurt we'd be liable for letting you use a faulty escalator."

"I'm not going to get hurt walking."

"Be that as it may, you can't walk up a broken escalator."

"What if I get hurt walking up the regular stairs? Wouldn't you be liable for that?"

"We're liable for everything. But at least you'd be using the stairs as they were intended to be used."

"Stairs are stairs," Jeremy said. "There's no difference between this unmoving escalator and those stairs."

"There is one crucial difference."

"What's that?"

"You're allowed to walk up those stairs."

"But the escalator is stairs," Jeremy said, exasperated.

"Not according to our insurance carrier it isn't."

Jeremy didn't want to get off to too bad a start with the security guard at his new office building, and used the sanctioned marble staircase a few yards over to go up to the bank of elevators. Getting upset over this kind of pettiness was inconsistent with the scale of his destiny, and he didn't give the escalator or the guard another thought.

He traveled to the eighth floor on the fastest elevator he'd ever been in. Slower elevators were better. They provided time enough to think, to prepare oneself for meeting new employers and coworkers. There was no chance for Jeremy to compose himself, to straighten his tie or even take a deep breath for relaxation of his nerves. The elevator doors opened and he exited. He walked down the hall, past several doors, until he found the sign that read: *RGP*. Underneath this, in smaller print, was the following: *Really Good Paper*. Jeremy opened the door.

The reception area consisted of a small black couch next to a desk. No one was sitting behind the desk, and Jeremy called out. "Hello?" A wall, six feet high, separated the reception desk from the rest of the space, which was in need of renovation. The wood floors were dull and light bulbs hung loosely from red and yellow wires from the twelve-foot ceiling—someone had apparently forgotten to purchase light fixtures, and it seemed that no more effort and thought had gone into decorating the place than naming it. Jeremy wandered past the reception area and into the main workroom. There were ten desks around the perimeter of the large room with narrow, iron-framed windows on its south side. At the far end of this room was a closed wood door, and Jeremy knocked.

"Come in," a man inside said.

Mr. Neenan shook Jeremy's hand and welcomed him to the Really Good Paper family. The company sold paper to institutions, like government agencies and schools and hospitals. They were currently expanding their retail sales force. There was quite a lot of money to be made in wedding and bar mitzvah invitations. Mr. Neenan had recently hired three people to make sure these invitations, which went out by the thousands each year, were on quality stock from his company. He loved paper and talked to Jeremy for ten minutes without pausing about the origins and ancient practices of the early paper makers. He finally got around to discussing the more practical matter of Jeremy's employment. Jeremy's brother Marc was a good customer of RGP, and Mr. Neenan was glad to be able to help Jeremy with a job. The first month would be a trial, but he was sure Jeremy could handle his vast responsibilities. If everything worked out there would be benefits and vacation days and opportunity for advancement.

Jeremy was politely thankful. He admitted to Mr. Neenan that he didn't know as much as he should about paper, but he was willing to study hard and learn all there was to know. His experience in sales was also unfortunately limited. But with a little training Jeremy was sure he could handle whatever region Mr. Neenan saw fit to allocate to him.

"I think there's been a misunderstanding," Mr. Neenan said. His bald white head was ringed by thin black hair and his eyes were bugged out, just enough to give him a more sinister appearance than his soothing voice indicated. He wore black slacks and boots for winter and a blue button-down shirt.

"I guess I don't get my own region right away," Jeremy said. "Not until after the trial period is over?"

"No, that's not it," Mr. Neenan said. "I don't have any sales positions open at the moment, and you're right, you don't have enough experience. I hired you to be our new receptionist."

"Oh."

"Your brother didn't tell you?" Mr. Neenan asked.

"No, he didn't."

"I'm sorry about the misunderstanding. But this is the only position I have that matches your background."

"I could sell," Jeremy said. "I could learn to sell."

"I'm sorry. What I need is a receptionist."

Jeremy wanted to run from the office, wanted to find his brother and demand an explanation. He was no receptionist. Did his brother think so little of his abilities? He wanted to say thank you but no thank you to Mr. Neenan. But Jeremy didn't flee reality's response to his unduly inflated career aspirations. The part of his brain in favor of keeping its promise to Mr. Valkof and paying the rent told the part of his brain insulted at this menial secretarial position that the specifics of the job were irrelevant—that people with destiny waiting for them like it waited for Jeremy needn't be concerned with how much of a living they earned or what demeaning tasks they performed to earn it.

"I would be happy to be your receptionist," Jeremy said.

Mr. Neenan was overjoyed, and showed Jeremy around—where the storage closet was, how to use the fax machine—all the essentials; the key to the hallway bathroom was on a hook next to the reception desk. Jeremy would need to answer the phone—it shouldn't be too difficult to keep up with incoming calls. Most of their business was conducted by outgoing calls, which would leave Jeremy free to file papers, run errands, send out packages, call for next-day delivery, and water the plants. The staff usually got in around nine-thirty, but Jeremy should come in at nine. Most nights he could leave by six. And, by the way, he should feel free to make coffee first thing in the morning—Mr. Neenan liked his with two sugars, one cream.

Jeremy answered the phone all morning: "Really Good Paper, Hello?" RGP had nine employees—seven salespeople, a distribution manager, and a bookkeeper. They were all wearing jeans and sweaters or buttoned shirts. Only Jeremy had on a tie. None of them had anything outside of hello to say to him when they arrived at work, and their verbosity did not increase as the day went on. Their friendships were already established, and Jeremy's desk was isolated. He ate lunch at half past noon by himself at a pizza shop two blocks away. Jeremy hadn't expected to leave his first day of work with a booming social life and the keys to a new car, but wouldn't have predicted he would be ignored and left to guard the key to the bathroom, either. He was aware that the world was full of suffering. He knew that many people had it worse than he did, that not only did destiny not call to most of them, but that some were starving or being ravaged by disease. Still, he thought there was nothing worse than having to eat lunch alone in a public place.

Sitting at his desk after lunch Jeremy heard a strange sound. It was coming from under the small black couch, the scraping of plastic against wood, and a soft squeaking noise. Jeremy didn't know what was causing the scratching. It wasn't very loud, and certainly no one in the other room could detect it. This was his chance to show his new boss that he was paying attention—all employers wanted detail-oriented employees. He reported to Mr. Neenan that the couch was emitting odd and disturbing noises. Jeremy was bold enough to suggest that perhaps the couch was structurally unsound, that a water pipe in the floor might be leaking, that the room or even the building itself might have a heretofore undiscovered defect.

"Let's take a look at what's making all that scratching," Mr. Neenan said. He walked to the reception area, got down on all fours, and pulled from under the couch a white plastic glue trap. Stuck in the trap, its hind legs in the thick yellow, was a small gray mouse, no bigger than the palm of a human hand. Mr. Neenan stood, still holding the trap, with the mouse dangling from its hind legs immersed in glue, and walked to the storage closet. The mouse was running in mid-air with its front paws but going nowhere. Its eyes searched everywhere for an escape but found none.

Jeremy followed Mr. Neenan and the mouse, silent. There were shelves of paper samples and magazines about selling and demographics. Mr. Neenan grabbed from the third shelf from the bottom a white plastic garbage bag with red drawstrings. He placed the mouse still attached to the trap into the bag and closed it tight. Setting the bag on the floor, he turned to Jeremy.

"Mice are a real problem," Mr. Neenan said. "They spread plagues and eat through electrical wires and are nuisances, leaving droppings everywhere. If left unchecked, they would overrun the human race. There isn't much we can do about it."

Then Mr. Neenan stomped with great speed on the part of the bag where the mouse was still squeaking and struggling to squirm free of the glue. His big black boot crushed it in an instant, and there was no time for a cry of injustice from the lifeless rodent.

Chapter 22

Tuesday came, and Wednesday, with no word from the man with the bushy mustache. Jeremy continued to answer the phone and water plants and make coffee. He was happy not to find any more mice in glue traps. Settling into a routine required no effort, and he soon knew everyone's name in the office and could direct calls without mistaking identities. He still set off the metal detector each morning and after returning from lunch each afternoon, and the white-haired security guard insisted each time on asking Jeremy if he had any weapons. Jeremy answered without fail that he had no weapons, that he didn't even know how to use a gun, but he remained patient with the guard. This was all the man had. His life was empty. He listened to the police scanner and patrolled the lobby of a building whose most controversial tenant made fake furs. If distrusting Jeremy because a nonexistent plate in his head set off the metal detector every day made the security guard feel more secure, who was Jeremy to take offense? People had done stranger things to give their lives meaning.

Static electricity occupied Jeremy's mind when he was sitting at his desk with nothing to do. When he wasn't planning his rise in the company or his destiny with the man with the bushy mustache or his strategy for winning back Brooke, Jeremy was trying to understand how electricity managed to follow him with such success. He thought maybe it was friction from the legs of his wool pants rubbing together when he walked, or that his shoes were not properly grounded. Whatever it was, the result was undeniable. He conducted electricity. Every time he opened the office's front door, at least a dozen times a day, the door's metal knob gave him a shock. Twice he even saw sparks. It wasn't a painful shock, just the standard static electricity to remind him that he was alive. Even though there was no real pain, instinct didn't allow him to voluntarily experience the electric pinch. Jeremy developed a kind of Pavlovian response, and by Wednesday, after being shocked twenty or thirty times by the same doorknob, he was unable to grab the knob and open the door without a ritual of preparation. He always tapped the plaster wall next to the door before reaching for the knob, as if this might alleviate the current flowing through him. It never did, and he continued to receive electric reminders of the laws of friction. He resorted to hiding his hand in his sleeve and opening the door with this cotton protection, the way one uses an oven mitt to remove a hot tray of food.

A note was waiting for Jeremy on his desk when he returned from his solitary lunch on Thursday: *Meet me at the park. Six pm. Come alone. —Eagle.* Jeremy told Mr. Neenan that he needed to leave work a few minutes early in order to see an old friend who was in town for just the night, and was surprised when Mr. Neenan not only didn't give him a hard time but told him to enjoy himself. Maybe Mr. Neenan wasn't a bad guy after all, even if he did crush mice beneath his black boot, even if his only love was the world of paper and his only dream one of expanding his domination of the industry until he had an empire of cotton bond and pastel parchment.

Jeremy arrived at the same park bench in Washington Square Park a few minutes after six. He felt that he'd been spending his whole life riding trains. Soon he would be on his way to greatness, his long search would be over, and all that he had endured to see it through would be fuel for his laughter. The man with the bushy mustache was waiting on the bench, wearing his black beret and his overcoat. With a look the man told Jeremy to say nothing—the benches might have ears. In silence Jeremy followed the man up a street and around a corner, then up two more blocks. They arrived at a brownstone and descended a flight of stairs. The man unlocked the door and gestured for Jeremy to enter. All doubts, all suspicions, all fears, were gone. He walked through the doorway and the man closed the door behind them.

The one bedroom apartment was small and neat. In the living room were red carpeting and a green couch and a long gray desk with a computer on it. A field of stars moved on the computer screen and two folding chairs were at the Formica dining table behind the couch. A black-framed reproduction of a famous work of art, of a hand drawing a hand, which was itself being drawn by the hand it was drawing, was on the wall above the computer monitor. The man with the bushy mustache removed his coat and beret and sat at the desk's chair, on wheels, and Jeremy sat on the couch. There was an awkward silence.

Finally Jeremy spoke. "So, here we are, at last."

"Yes," the man with the bushy mustache said. "At last."

"You didn't tell me much last Friday. I have to confess, I'm excited about learning what this is all about."

"The conditions are better today."

"So you can answer my questions?"

"No one can interfere. We are safe from eavesdroppers."

"Good," Jeremy said. "How many members are there? Who else has the gold eagle with the outstretched wings?"

"Just you. No one else."

"But you told me only to trust those wearing the eagle."

"I told you that so you wouldn't fall for any of their stories, in case they came to see you," the man said.

"Who are 'they?'"

"The CIA, NASA, other organizations. They'd love to get their hands on me."

"Why?" Jeremy asked.

"You'll understand soon."

"Why were you following me?"

"Did you ever know something?" the man asked. "I mean, something that you had no reason to know but you were no less certain for your lack of proof?"

They were words Jeremy could have spoken about himself—they summed up his understanding of his destiny nicely. He nodded in agreement.

"I discovered you by accident. I was walking along and there you were. Something told me that you were what I needed for my work, and I followed you to make sure. I know that might sound crazy. I'd never followed anyone before. For a while I thought I'd lost it."

"I understand how you felt. I'd never been followed before. But it made sense that I was being followed, even if to other people it might be crazy." They were birds of a feather. "What work do you need my help for?"

"Let me try to explain it to you," the man said.

Jeremy had waited months for this, and listened intently.

"I'm an actuary. That's what I do for a living."

"What's an actuary?" Jeremy asked. It sounded important.

"I specialize in math, in statistics and probability. I work for an insurance company."

"I don't know anything about insurance."

"This isn't about insurance," the man said. "The first thing you learn in my field, if you're paying attention, is that insurance is a myth. We specialize in predicting things. What's the probability of being hit by lightning? Or dying in a car crash? Or being eaten alive by fire ants? You'd be surprised how many deaths each year are attributed to those bastards."

"Sounds painful."

"I wouldn't know. But I do know that there are more ways to die now than ever before. You heard of that house hit by frozen waste from a passing airplane? We cure diseases but people around the world are still dying from them. We eliminate smallpox and then throw blocks of blue ice out of planes at people."

"It isn't good," Jeremy said.

"That's right. The problem is that we don't predict anything at all. We can't predict. You're a young man. You look healthy. You should live a long life. But you might not make it through the week. Someone could shoot you, a meteorite could come crashing down on your head, your heart might just quit on you like it did for those basketball players. There's no way to know what's going to happen."

"I'm pretty careful."

"Careful has nothing to do with it. This planet doesn't let you be careful. Lightning doesn't care if you always buckle up; criminals don't care if you're a nonsmoker. Do you know how many people drowned in their cars last year because of overflowing rivers? This world doesn't have mercy."

"It *is* dangerous," Jeremy said.

"My birth certificate says I was born in 1961, but I was really born on July 21, 1969." The man spoke rapidly now, possessed by the idea he wanted to get across. "The Eagle has landed. The Eagle has landed. That's what they said when they landed on the moon."

"What does the moon have to do with anything?"

"Sit in this chair," the man said, standing and offering the black office chair to Jeremy. "Sit. You'll understand in a minute."

Jeremy sat in the chair. It was comfortable, with armrests on either side. "What should I do?"

"Spin," the man said.

"Spin?" Jeremy asked.

"Use your feet. Push yourself faster and faster."

Jeremy started to spin.

"Faster," the man said, and he began spinning the chair to help Jeremy gain speed.

Jeremy was turning as fast as the chair's swivel allowed. The room passed before his eyes over and over as he spun.

"When I tell you to," the man said, "put your feet down and stop… Now."

Jeremy stopped the spinning with his feet.

"Do you see?" the man asked, excited for Jeremy's discovery.

"No," Jeremy said.
"How do you feel?" the man asked.
"A little dizzy."
"Exactly. The Eagle has landed."
"I don't know about the eagle landing," Jeremy said. "I'm just a little dizzy."
"That's what it's like on the moon."
"Huh?"
"Let me show you," the man said, walking toward the bedroom.
"What's in there?"
"The answer," the man said.
"What answer?"
"To the question. Follow me."

The bedroom had no bed, only a narrow army cot. A wood crate covered with tin foil, big enough for a person to almost stand inside at full height, was in the center of the room, on a foot-high platform. Three car batteries with wires running from them to the silver-covered box were on the red carpet. The batteries were all connected to a generator, which was not running. A flexible tube ran from the generator's exhaust to the window, where it remained due to several layers of gray duct tape. Nothing else was in the room.

"This is it," the man with the bushy mustache said.
"What is it?"
"The cure."
"The cure for what?" Jeremy asked.
"For the world. It's like spinning on a chair. When you spin nothing bothers you. You're like the Eagle landing. You're not part of the planet. You're away from the world. No one can touch you. But the spinning has to stop even-

tually, and then the world comes rushing back in. Do you understand?"

"Kind of." Jeremy did know that one couldn't spin on chairs forever.

"We're stuck in this box," the man said. "This world is a box, our jobs are boxes, money another box, probability and statistics also boxes. Don't you see? I've built a box that frees us from the box."

"I don't understand."

"Get in the box and I'll show you."

"I don't want to get in that box," Jeremy said. "It looks dangerous."

"You're in a box already. This box will free you."

"What will happen to me in there?"

"I read a comic book when I was a kid, about a man who could walk through walls. He could throw off the density of the world and become intangible, like a ghost. Nothing could hurt him. Bullets, knives, rocks falling from the sky. He wasn't part of the physical world. He was safe."

"I remember that comic," Jeremy said. "But it wasn't a man, it was an android."

"Then you understand," the man said. "This tin box can make you untouchable. Think of living without fear. We'll be of this world, but not in the world. I made the machine, that was my destiny. But something told me, the second I saw you, that it was your destiny to be the first untouchable man."

"I don't know anything about science, but I don't see what a few batteries hooked up to aluminum foil is going to do."

"It'll work."

"Besides, I don't want to be untouchable."

"Of course you do," the man said. "We all do."

"No, really, I don't," Jeremy said.

"This changes things... Will you operate the batteries for me? I need to be in the box when the power is turned on."

"It doesn't look safe."

"It's safe."

"I can't help you," Jeremy said.

"How will I get home?"

"We're in your apartment."

"Not here," the man said. "Home." He stepped out of the bedroom doorway and pointed to the computer screen with the drifting stars.

"I still don't understand," Jeremy said.

"My name is Eagle. And I am from the moon."

"From the moon?"

"I was brought here by mistake," he said. "This planet isn't mine. I need to free myself of this solid body so I can go home."

"You're from the moon?"

"Ever since I heard those words, 'The Eagle has landed,' I've been away from home. I need your help to go back."

"Maybe you should see a doctor," Jeremy said.

"I don't need a doctor. There's nothing wrong with me. The planet needs a doctor. I just need you to throw that switch."

"I can't help you."

"You have to," the man said.

"No. Why don't we go see a doctor?"

"You can't leave me here. I'm trapped on earth. This isn't my world. I don't belong here."

"I'm sorry."

"You're not leaving until you help me."

"I'm going," Jeremy said, and walked out of the bedroom.

There came a crashing from the room. Jeremy ran back to the doorway, and saw the man with the bushy mustache, in his dark suit and red tie, swinging a car battery over his head by its wires, like a gladiator, smashing it into the foil-covered box. He was yelling at the box, or himself, "You won't trap me!"

Jeremy was afraid to get any closer, and shouted from the doorway, "You're gonna kill yourself!"

The man released the battery and it sailed into the wall next to Jeremy, shattering. Battery acid leaked from its cracked container. The man picked up another battery, and Jeremy didn't wait to see what his plans were for it, running out of the apartment and to a payphone a block away.

He called the police and stood in the cold darkness for ten minutes until he saw two cars with flashing lights pull up. Four officers went down into the brownstone. Jeremy didn't stay to see them leading the man with the bushy mustache out. He unpinned his eagle with outstretched wings and dropped it in a trashcan; he'd had enough of fool's gold.

Chapter 23

Early Friday afternoon Jeremy went to Strawberry Dreams to see Brooke. When he reached for the doorknob to leave his office, he resisted the impulse to first touch the wall or to cover his hand with his sleeve. He was determined not to let a little shock of electricity tame him like some broken dog. He closed his bare hand around the metal knob. It was cold and smooth, and there were no flying sparks or dimming lights attributable to his conductive powers.

Jeremy had to see Brooke. She was all he had left. He had stopped trying to make sense of the man with the bushy mustache. It was hard to fault the man's desperate need to disown this world. The city, really the people in the city, really the people everywhere, could take their toll on a human heart. Living on the moon had its advantages. Jeremy was beginning to see everything, all of his experiences, his entire life to this point, in a new light. All the people he had encountered, all the shouting and the screaming and the crying, the pretend guns and the deadly forks and the spraying acid, the pushers and the detectives and the karate poses and the security guards, were all the same. They were just trying to live. They were searching, but what for they hadn't a clue. They were lost. And so was Jeremy.

He didn't know what he'd expected to find in himself, what the man with the bushy mustache could have done or said that would have created order out of the chaos of Jeremy's existence. The truth of the man's purpose didn't live up to the mystery, didn't reveal things about Jeremy's own character he'd been waiting a lifetime to discover were true. Being followed had been enough. It was the indication of his importance, not the specifics, that he'd come to value. Now he had neither. He'd been wrong about his job—twice. He was wrong about his destiny. His refusal to see himself through any but the most distorted mirror had led him astray. All he had was Brooke. And he didn't even have her.

Snow was falling and the sidewalk was covered with thin white powder. The first snowfall was always the best, until the buses and cars turned the pure alabaster into black slush. Strawberry Dreams was the same as the last time he'd visited, just over a week earlier to ask Brooke out for that first date. Jeremy didn't know why he expected it to look different. So much had happened to him—he'd changed since then. She was behind the counter, the same as always, smiling and looking like something even people from the moon might stay on earth for. Jeremy walked to the counter.

"Hi," he said.

Brooke looked up. "What are you doing here?" For the first time since he saw her back on that autumn day, she wasn't smiling.

"You didn't ask me what my strawberry dream was," Jeremy said.

"I don't think you're supposed to be here," she said. "I think we have a court order that says you can't come within twenty-five yards of the place."

"Twenty-five?" Jeremy asked. "The rest of my restraining orders are for a hundred. Or is it fifty? There are really too many to keep track with any accuracy."

"You're not supposed to be here," she said.

"I'm not supposed to be anywhere. Pretty soon I won't be allowed to leave my apartment."

"You should go," Brooke said.

"I just wanted to give you this," Jeremy said, handing her a lavender envelope.

"What is it?"

"Open it."

She opened it. Inside was a greeting card, on its cover a happy snowman offering flowers. She read the poem out loud:

> *your smile melts the winter's snow,*
> *your voice scares the clouds away,*
> *the sun shines and flowers grow*
> *for you on Valentine's Day!*

"It isn't Valentine's yet," she said. "It isn't even Christmas for almost another week."

"I know," Jeremy said. "But it's the only card I have. And it made me think of you."

"I don't like the idea of you thinking of me."

"Brooke, I love you."

"You're crazy."

"I am a lot of things," Jeremy said. "But I know crazy. And I'm not crazy."

"If you're not crazy then you're nuts," she said.

"I know I haven't exactly done all the right things—"

"All the right things? You lie to me for months, pretending to like strawberries, and then you almost kill yourself on our date. I've been on bad dates. One guy wanted me to pay for everything, another couldn't keep his hands off me, but you're the first to try to kill himself with fruit."

"I wasn't trying to kill myself."

"You lied to me, Jeremy. You came into the boutique every day and lied to me."

"I know."

"You were stalking me. I was at work, and you came everyday to stalk me."

"I just thought you had a pretty smile. Isn't there any way you can forgive me?"

"I don't think so," she said. "You're not who I thought you were."

"I'm not who I thought I was either. And you're the only thing I have left in my life."

"I'm sorry," Brooke said.

"Do you have a pen?" Jeremy asked. "And a sheet of paper?"

"Why?"

"Can I borrow a pen and paper, please?"

Brooke handed him a pen and a small napkin with a graphic of King Strawberry on his golden couch. Jeremy wrote his phone number and gave her the napkin.

"If you change your mind," he said, "call me."

"I'm not going to change my mind."

"I can only apologize so much," Jeremy said. "I won't bother you again. I won't chase anymore. I'm making some changes in my life. I want you to be a part of it, but I can't go on living the way I've been. If you're going to throw out my number, please wait till I leave."

Brooke tucked the napkin into the pocket of her apron.

"Thank you," Jeremy said, and smiled at her. He owed her that. Then he walked out of Strawberry Dreams and her life, forever.

The snow was falling hard and fast, with an inch already on the ground. Jeremy removed his coat after wiping his feet and sat at his desk. He answered phones. That's all he did. He wasn't on the edge of history, as the man with the bushy mustache had told him once in the park. He wasn't about to stumble onto anything big. He was just a man, no different from any other.

There was a squeaking noise from under the couch. Jeremy crawled and put his ear to the floor. He could see a gray mouse, a tiny thing with a long tail, stuck in the glue-filled plastic trap. Jeremy jumped up and checked the main workroom. Most of the office was out to lunch, and two people ate Chinese food out of white cartons. Jeremy grabbed a utility knife and a paper bag from the supply cabinet in the storage closet, and asked them to watch the phones for a few minutes. He knelt once again next to the couch in the reception area, and pulled the glue trap out. He rushed it into the paper bag, and went to the bathroom in the hallway.

The mouse's front legs were stuck, but not very deep. Jeremy held the mouse still. It tried to squirm away, but his grip was firm. The mouse's fur was as soft as a dog's or a cat's. With the sharp edge of the utility knife he cut the glue away, carving around the mouse's legs until they were no longer trapped. He put the knife in his pocket and buried the glue trap in the garbage under paper towels, so no one would know he had interfered. He placed the mouse in the paper bag. The mouse was still. Jeremy ripped a few tiny holes in the bag for air, and took the elevator down.

He descended the marble stairs and tried to pass the security guard quickly, but the guard saw him coming and stepped in front of Jeremy.

"What's in the bag?" the guard asked.

"Nothing important," Jeremy said.

"What's your hurry?"

"No hurry."

"You're not even wearing a coat," the guard said.

Jeremy didn't realize he had forgotten his coat until the guard pointed it out. "Just want to enjoy the snow."

"You have no coat and you're rushing out of here with a bag. My guess is you stole something. Office supplies, maybe?"

"I didn't steal anything."

"Why don't you show me what's in the bag, then?" the guard asked.

"I'm not going to show you what's in this bag," Jeremy said. "I work here, in this building. I'm tired of playing your game. Everyone's game. You work here, for me, in the building I work in. I'm not your toy. You can't harass me every time you feel like playing cops and robbers. If you don't start treating me with a little respect I'm going to complain to building management."

"Don't be mad at me just because you have a plate in your head," the guard said. But he stood aside and let Jeremy and his bag of stolen goods pass.

Jeremy walked down the block, not feeling the cold or the driving snow. He turned up a side street, the closest thing to an alley this part of Manhattan offered. Only now did he have some understanding of what it all meant. The truth was, he wasn't destined for big things. Which didn't mean that destiny ignored him entirely. He was destined for little things. And that was enough.

Jeremy knelt and opened the bag. Without hesitation the mouse scurried out into the sun reflecting off the fresh white, its panicked feet making shuffling prints in the snow. Within seconds any trace of the mouse's trail was covered by still more flakes. The mouse ran along the brick wall and then was gone, finding its way into a crevice or hole in some back door. Jeremy didn't know if its chances were better where it was now. Perhaps it would meet other mice—maybe it would find food and avoid for a time the fate it had escaped this afternoon. Perhaps it would be trapped again tomorrow. But today, anyway, it was free.

A Note about the Author

Scott Stein was born in New York in 1971, grew up in Bayside, Queens, has lived on Manhattan's Upper and Lower East Sides, and now lives outside of Philadelphia with his wife. His short fiction has been published in *The G.W. Review*, *Art Times*, and *Liberty*. He is an Assistant Professor at Drexel University, and taught Creative Writing and English Composition at Cheyney University of Pennsylvania. As the founder and editor of *When Falls the Coliseum: a journal of American culture (or lack thereof)*, he regularly publishes humor, fiction, and opinion by writers from across the United States at www.wfthecoliseum.com. He received his BA and MFA from the University of Miami and his MA from New York University. This is his first novel.

LOST was designed and composed by
Free Reign Press, Inc. in Langhorne, PA.

www.freereignpress.com